"Read in the order written, [the Brandstetter mysteries] are remarkably linked through symbol, incident, and character, to the point that one sees them as a single, multi-volume novel, by which one may learn a great deal about what it means to be homosexual and male in modern America."

—*The New Republic*

"Hansen is quite simply the most exciting and effective writer of the classic California private-eye novel working today."

—*Los Angeles Times*

"No one in the history of the detective novel has had the daring to do what Joseph Hansen has done: make his private eye a homosexual ... who is both a first-rate investigator and one of the most interesting series characters in the history of the genre."

—**David Geherin,**
The American Private Eye

"The first thing I ever read by Joseph Hansen was *Fadeout* (1970). It's the seminal novel in a mystery series about a smart, tough, uncompromising insurance investigator by the name of David Brandstetter. He is a Korean War vet and ruggedly masculine. He's educated, principled, compassionate—but willing and able to use violence when nothing else works. He represents the (then) new breed of PI—the post-World War II private investigator. There are no bottles of rye in Dave's desk, there are no sleazy secrets in his past, and the dames don't much tend to throw themselves at him. He is neither tarnished nor afraid. Oh, and one other thing. He's gay. ... He was not the first gay detective to hit mainstream crime fiction, but he was the first normal gay detective, and that—as the poet said —has made all the difference."

—**Josh Lanyon,**
from *The Golden Age of Gay Fiction*

DEATH CLAIMS

DEATH CLAIMS

JOSEPH HANSEN

A DAVE BRANDSTETTER NOVEL

SYNDICATE BOOKS
NEW YORK

First published in 1973
by Harper and Row

This edition published in 2021
by Syndicate Books
www.syndicatebooks.com

Distributed by
Soho Press, Inc.
227 W 17th Street
New York, NY 10011

Copyright © 1973 The Estate of Joseph Hansen

ISBN 978-1-68199-049-1
eISBN 978-1-68199-047-7

Printed in the United States of America

10 9 8 7 6 5 4 3 2 1

1

ARENA BLANCA WAS right. The sand that bracketed the little bay was so white it hurt the eyes. A scatter of old frame houses edged the sand, narrow, high-shouldered, flat-roofed. It didn't help that they were gay with new paint— yellow, blue, lavender. They looked bleak in the winter sun. Above them gulls sheared a sky cheerful as new denim. The bay glinted like blue tile. The small craft at anchor might have been dabbed there by Raoul Dufy. It was still bleak. So were the rain-greened hills that shut the place off. He drove down out of them bleakly.

The bleakness was in him. After only three months he and Doug were coming apart. The dead were doing it—Doug's dead, a French boy, skull shattered at a sun-blaze bend on the raceway at Le Mans; his own dead, a graying boy interior decorator, eaten out by cancer in a white nightmare hospital. He and Doug clung tight, but the dead crept cold between them. Neither he nor Doug knew how to bury them and in their constant presence they treated each other with the terrible, empty gentleness people substitute for love at funerals. It was no way to live and they weren't living.

Where the road reached the beach a clump of country mailboxes leaned together, clumsy tin flowers, each a different color, their props deep in tough dune grass. The box labeled STANNARD was pink, which he guessed meant it belonged to the house on the left, out at the point. He dug a cigarette from his jacket, poked the dash lighter, turned the wheel. The road had been blacktopped but not lately. Sand and grass were reclaiming it. Near the point it was no more than ruts. Wind got to it here, spray, sometimes even surf—shell crunched under the tires, a thin litter of driftwood.

The first level of the pink house was car stalls. The sagging door was up. A fifties Ford station wagon waited inside, scabbing its pink paint. The lighter clicked, he started the cigarette and left his car in the road. It wouldn't be blocking traffic. He climbed wooden outside stairs to a corner of deck and a door. Salt crusted the bell button, but it worked. He heard a buzz. A pan clattered. Quick footsteps shook the place. The door jerked open. A girl said shrilly:

"Where have you been? Couldn't you phone? I—"

She broke off. He'd been wrong—she wasn't a girl. Maybe last year she had been. She was a woman now. She tried for a smile, but the lines it made beside her mouth said strain, not happiness. Something had dulled her eyes to the faded blue of the man's workshirt she'd tucked into a dungaree skirt. No stockings, loafers with broken stitches. Her hands were wet and soapy. She wiped them on the skirt and brushed blonde hair off her forehead.

"I'm sorry," she said. "I was expecting someone else. Who are you?"

"My name is David Brandstetter. I'm a claims investigator for Medallion Life Insurance Company." He handed her a card. She didn't glance at it. Her eyes were anxious on his face. He said, "I'm looking for Peter Oats. Does he live here?"

"Investigator?" The word came out frayed. "Oh, no. Don't tell me there's something wrong with John's insurance. That was the one thing he—"

"The insurance is all right," Dave said. "May I talk to Peter Oats?"

"He's not here." Her shoulders slumped. "I wish he were. I can't find him. He doesn't even know his father's dead." The word hurt her to say. She bit her lip and blinked back tears. "Look, Mr. Brand—?" The name had gotten away from her. It got away from most people the first time.

He repeated it. "And your name is Stannard?"

"April." She nodded. "Look—come in. Maybe I can help." Her laugh was forlorn. "Maybe you can help me. The police don't seem to care." She turned from the door. "Excuse how things look."

He couldn't see after the sun-dazzle outside. Then he heard the squeak of little pulleys. Drapes parted, flowered drapes, bleached at the pleats. The front wall was glass for the view of the bay. It was salt-misted, but it let him see the room. Neglected. Dust blurred the spooled maple of furniture that was old but used to better care. The faded chintz slipcovers needed straightening. Threads of cobweb spanned lampshades. And on a coffee table stood plates soiled from a meal eaten days ago—canned roast-beef hash, ketchup—dregs of coffee in cups, half a glass of dead, varnishy liquid, a drink unfinished that never would be finished.

"Sit down," she said. "I'll get us coffee."

He dropped on to the couch and his knee nudged a trio of books balanced on a corner of the coffee table. Heavy matched folios, handsome, in full tree calf, the boards unwarped, the grain scrupulously preserved, with the kind of patina that brings up the price of old violins. Eighteenth century, seventeenth? He reached for them, but she got them first.

"Here, let me put those out of your way." Shelving lined two walls, floor to ceiling, crowded. She couldn't find a gap for the three big volumes. "That's odd. I don't remember these." She stood two of them on the floor to lean against the lower shelves, opened the third and gave a little whistle.

"*Cook's Voyages*. A first edition." She frowned for a second, then shrugged, set it down and bent across Dave to gather up the plates, cups, glass. And a pocket-creased envelope—British stamp, elegant engraved letterhead. "I haven't done a thing," she said. "I'm ashamed. Everything's just the way he left it." She went off, but she raised her voice while she rattled china in the kitchen. "If Peter had been here, I'd have pulled myself together. As it was, I couldn't bear it. I just let down. Until today. Today I've been trying to clean up." She brought coffee in cups that suited the room—flowery, fragile, feminine. Not, he thought, like this girl. She sat in a wing chair. "Began with the kitchen. I'm not ready for this room yet. Not without someone in it besides me."

"I understand." He meant he remembered.

"I was fine at the inquest. People. Alone, I haven't been fine. Not fine at all." She blew at the vapor curling on her coffee. "I lost my mother last winter. Now John. I wasn't ready for it."

"Was he a relative?"

Her smile was wan, the corner of a smile. "We were lovers. We were going to be married. When his divorce was final. What did you want to ask Peter?"

"How old are you, Miss Stannard?"

"Twenty-four, and John was forty-nine." Her chin lifted, her eyes cleared. "And his poor body was a mass of scars. And he'd lost everything he'd worked a lifetime for— business, home, money. But I loved him. He was the finest human being I ever knew or ever expect to know." Her words snagged on tears and she drank coffee, blinking. When she'd steadied, she shook her head and frowned. "I suppose it must have been the pain. They said at the inquest he'd been taking morphine. He never told me. You see how he was?"

"Are you suggesting"—Dave set the pansy-painted cup in the pansy-painted saucer—"he killed himself?"

"No, not really. We were so happy. It's just that"—her shoulders moved—"I don't have any explanation for what happened. He wouldn't go to swim in the rain. It doesn't make sense. Yes, he did swim at night. He didn't want to be seen. He was worried that the scars would shock people, repel them, offend them. He always swam at night. But not in the rain."

A pair of china parakeets billed on the frilly rim of an ashtray stuffed with dusty butts, three different brands of filter-tips—Kent, Marlboro, Tareyton. Dave stubbed out his cigarette among them. "You weren't here?"

She gave her head a quick shake. "It was one of those—I thought—lucky days when I got a call to work. I'd been hunting a job, you might say desperately, for weeks. But I'd only gotten this off-and-on thing at Bancroft's. Books are all I know. I've been into books since I was, like, four. I didn't have to have a job at college, but I was in the bookstore so much I guess they figured they'd better pay me." Faint smile. "Afterward I went to work for John. That was how we—came to know each other." Her face went still with remembering for a moment. Then she took a breath. "Anyway, one of Bancroft's clerks was out with flu and would I come in for the afternoon and evening? We were down to half a jar of peanut butter. I went."

"To the branch in El Molino?"

"No, worse luck. The main one, the big one, on Vine in Hollywood. Not exactly in the neighborhood." She breathed a rueful little laugh. "And the car isn't exactly new. It was Mother's. A bangwagon."

"It could use some paint," Dave said.

"It could use a lot of things. Mother kept it just for this place, summers. My own I sold. To help pay John's doctor bills. His went for the same reason, long ago. So you drive, when you drive, prayerfully. I got there all right, but, coming home, the fan belt broke. On the coast road, a long way between filling stations. It was late when I got back. And John wasn't here. I didn't know what to think. He never left the place except to drive with me to the shopping center up the highway. It would be an awfully long walk."

"You didn't find him that night," Dave said.

She tilted her head. "You already know. How?"

"I read the transcript of the inquest."

Her clear forehead creased. "Why?"

He gave her half a smile and told her half the truth. "Routine. It's what they pay me for."

"But now you're here." She sat still, guarded.

"I'm here because insurance companies don't much care for verdicts like 'death by misadventure'. You found him in the morning?"

"I looked that night. Put on a raincoat and went down to the beach, calling him. My flashlight's old and feeble, but I might have found him. I didn't go clear to the point. I guess I couldn't really believe he'd be out there drowned. Too melodramatic. Things like that don't happen."

"You didn't think of calling the police?"

"That's a little melodramatic too, isn't it?"

"Maybe. What about his friends?"

Her laugh was scornful. "He had no friends. A lot of people knew him. He knew a lot of people. He thought of them as friends. He was theirs. They were only customers. He gave out all this warmth, charm, humor. I wish you'd known him. A nice man, a beautiful man, all the way through. He remembered them, all their names, the subjects they were interested in, titles, authors. He was a good bookman, but more than that, a good man—period. Anything personal they'd ever told him—setbacks, advances, ailments, wives, children, dogs, cats—he remembered. He really cared. Only a handful ever showed up at the hospital. And most of them only once." It still angered her. "It was a lesson in human nature he didn't deserve." She looked too young for it herself, slender and pale against the faded flower fabric of the wing chair. "I brought him down here afterward. If any of them bothered to find out, they didn't give any evidence of it. Luckily, he didn't care by then. We had each other. It was all either of us wanted."

"What about his partner? Didn't he come?"

"Charles?" She shook her head. Her smile was wan. "I'm afraid he's jealous. Of me. Poor Charles."

"What made you look for John in the morning?"

"I didn't." Color came to her face. "I walked on the beach again, but not looking for him. You see, I'd made up a story by then, sitting here, waiting. I decided Peter had come and they'd gone off together. To look at whatever place Peter was living."

"Does Peter own a car?"

"No, but other things said Peter. There were two plates for supper, two cups but only one glass. Peter doesn't drink—he only just turned twenty-one. Also, when he moved out he left his guitar. And it was gone from his room. Anyway, who else could it be but Peter? I didn't think about the car. Kids borrow cars. But of course, there was a big flaw in my story. John would have left a note for me and there was no note. Still—I had to believe something."

"Something non-melodramatic," Dave said.

She gave a little nod. "And by morning it had become absolutely true to me. And I was hurt. If John had tried to phone before I got home, to explain he was staying over with Peter on account of the rain, he could have kept phoning till he got me. Or Peter could have, if John was too tired—he could tire suddenly. So I was feeling sorry for myself. Taken for granted. Abused. And when it got daylight and the phone just sat there and I couldn't bear to look at it anymore and I couldn't bear the emptiness of this place without him, I went down and walked on the beach again. It was still raining, but not hard—gentle, sifting. Gray, you know? Mournful?" She breathed a wry laugh at herself. "Like a scene from a film. Young girl alone on empty beach, shivering, forsaken, deeply hurt. In the rain, with the sad gulls crying. Romantic." Her mouth tightened in a grim crooked line. "Until I found him." She spoke it harshly and her hand shook when she tried to drink from the cup. "The dead are terrible," she said. "They

7

won't help you at all. No matter how you loved them. No matter how they loved you."

She was right and he didn't want to think about it. He said, "Wasn't Peter in the way?"

2

SHE STIFFENED. "I don't understand you."

"Of the love you keep talking about," Dave said. "Yours and John Oats's. This isn't a very big house. Wasn't a college boy underfoot?"

She set down her cup. Too fast. Coffee tilted into the saucer. She stood up. "I don't think you're going to help me," she said coldly.

Dave stood up too. "I'm going to find him. That's what you want, isn't it?"

She watched him distrustfully. "I did. Do I now? What's your reason for wanting to find him?"

"A piece of mail from my company arrived here the day after his father drowned. Addressed to John Oats. Did you open it?"

She shook her head. "I didn't even collect the mail—not for days. Then I got to thinking there might be word from Peter and I made myself look. There wasn't any word from Peter. I didn't open the rest."

"Is it here somewhere?"

A door broke the wall of shelves. She went out through it and came back with envelopes and put them into his hands. They felt dusty. He shuffled them. Phone bill. Book-auction catalog. There it was—gold medallion in the corner. He held it out to her. Frowning, she tore it open and took out the folded sheets. She blinked at them, then at him.

"It's some sort of form," she said. "The letter says to fill it out and return it."

"He phoned Medallion the morning of the day he drowned. He said he wanted to change the beneficiary of his life insurance. It's a simple procedure. The clerk sent him the necessary papers."

She stared at him for a moment, not understanding. Then her eyes widened. She dropped into the chair. Her tongue touched her lips. The words came out a whisper. "Peter was the beneficiary."

"Does that answer your question?"

"No." She moved her head from side to side. Slow. Stricken. "Oh, no. You can't believe Peter would kill his father. Oh, you don't know him. You didn't know John. You don't know what they meant to each other. You don't know—"

"I know he'd been struck on the head."

"By the rocks!" She shouted it. "The surf smashes on those rocks in a storm. It picked him up and—it's in the coroner's report." Her hands were clenched, the knuckles white as the papers they crumpled. "Why can't you believe the coroner? He's seen more drowned men than you have. John's lungs were full of water."

"I didn't say the blow on the head killed him. He drowned. I believe the coroner." He gave her a thin smile. "I believe him the way you do—uneasily. You can't figure John Oats going to swim in the rain."

"The police believe him," she argued.

"You told me yourself the police don't care. They've got a verdict that doesn't involve them. It's not their problem anymore. It's still my problem." He lit a cigarette. "He could have been knocked unconscious here in this room, undressed and dragged down to the beach and into the water."

"Not by Peter." Her face set stubbornly. "He couldn't, he wouldn't. Why would he?"

"For twenty thousand dollars." Dave walked to the fogged glass wall. A trawler inched along the far blue edge of the horizon. "You say he had supper with his father. Maybe his father told him he was changing beneficiaries. Did Peter need twenty thousand dollars?"

"No. Whatever for?"

"I'd like to ask him." Dave turned. "Why don't you know where he is? Weren't you on speaking terms?"

She flushed. "I invited Peter down here to live. Before his father, even. I felt sorry for him. He was miserable with his mother. Especially after she—" Her voice dropped. "After she did what she did. But they never got along. While John was in the house it was, well, at least possible. With John in the hospital, he simply couldn't take it. There was room here. I said, 'Stay at the beach place.' I was still living at the family house then. In time I sold it. Had to. There were so many bills, such huge bills."

"Not yours, though. John Oats's—right?"

She nodded. "There was operation after operation. Specialists. Skin grafts. Hideous. There were so many times he thought he couldn't take it anymore, when he was ready to give up, when he just wanted to be allowed to die and get it over with."

"So Peter came to live here?" Dave bent at the table to use the parakeet ashtray. "Then you came. And finally you brought John Oats when he was released from the hospital. And Peter moved out."

"No. John was here in time for Christmas. Peter didn't move out till—what?—two, three weeks ago. He'd had a birthday. He'd graduated from El Molino State."

"You don't know where he went. Do you know why?"

"Well, it wasn't because he was underfoot. When he wasn't at school, he was at the El Molino Stage. It's the community little theater. But even if he hadn't been, he wasn't childish. He was happy for John and me. Yes, it's a small place. Yes, John and I slept together. It's not the nineteenth century anymore, Mr. Brandstetter. Especially not to people under twenty-one."

"I'll have to change my calendar," Dave said. "The one with the kittens and the satin bows." He picked up his cup and swallowed some coffee. "If you were getting along with him, why didn't he tell you his reason for going? He had to say something."

"I wasn't here for him to say anything to. I was working again. He didn't come home the night before. Next evening when I got here he'd moved out."

"Just like that. What did his father say?"

She breathed in sharply. "Look, Mr. Brandstetter, suppose you leave now. I really don't think I have to answer your questions. I've told the police all about this. Captain Campos. If you really feel you need to know, I'm sure his records will be open to you, just as the inquest transcript was." She stood up.

"You don't want to send me to the police, Miss Stannard." He looked at her hard and straight. "Not unless you've got it in for Peter for some reason. See, they don't know yet that John Oats was about to erase Peter as his beneficiary."

Her mouth was a tight line for a minute. Then she went to the window. Her words came to him flattened by the glass. "John didn't say anything. 'I don't want to discuss it,' was all. He drank more than usual that evening. I thought I could get an explanation from him then. I couldn't."

"Was he angry?"

She turned. "Not angry. Depressed. Terribly. He loved Peter. They'd gone through so much together. That woman was such a bitch. I don't think either of them could have made it alone. They'd been a team. Now, suddenly they weren't a team anymore."

"He had another woman now." Dave gave her a smile. "One who wasn't a bitch."

She returned the smile, but dimly. "Maybe. I'm afraid I acted like one right then. I hated for him to be so unhappy. I hated Peter for having done it to him. I guess I was jealous too. It was the first time he'd ever shut me out that way. We'd always been open with each other. But he'd suffered so much I couldn't turn on him. Instead I said a lot of harsh things about Peter. John didn't respond right. He just stared at me. Sad. So sad." She shivered, clutched herself, turned back to the window.

"Maybe he brooded about the boy." Dave bent to twist out his cigarette. "Maybe he could have walked into the surf in the rain, not wanting to come out."

She turned back, stung. "I was here."

"Not that day. It might have been too long for him. There are days like that."

"No. He wouldn't. Not after the fight he'd put up to stay alive. Not after the way I'd fought to keep him alive. He wouldn't. He wouldn't do it to me."

Dave moved to the shelves, prying reading glasses out of his jacket pocket. The books were ninety percent old. Some of them respectably, some just shabbily. But they all had a chosen look. He put the glasses on. "I don't know what sent him to the hospital."

"Burns. They'd bought a new house. Not new, but expensive. Not his idea. Eve's. That was how she was. Never satisfied. Always asking him for more, more."

"Some men need that," Dave said, "or think they do." He took down a book in dark-blue cloth with worn gold bars stamped across the thick spine. *Look Homeward, Angel.* Scribner, 1929. The "A" below the copyright data made it a first edition. "He stayed with her."

She let that pass. "It was a hillside house, with a storage room under it on the down slope at the back. He wanted to use it for books. There were always more than the shop could hold. It's the same with every bookseller. The car sits rusting in the street because the garage is filled with books."

He set the Thomas Wolfe book back. There were others beside it—*Of Time and the River*, stocky black and green, *From Death to Morning*, soft coffee brown.

"There were grease stains on the cement floor and John wanted to be able to set books down there while he arranged them on the shelves he was going to build in.

And so—" The tough dungaree of her skirt whistled against the chintz as she sat down again. "He got a can of gasoline and was going to scrub up the grease stains. The weather was cold. The door and windows were shut. The gas hot-water heater was in the corner. And when he splashed the stuff around, either the gas itself touched the pilot flame or maybe just the fumes. Anyway, in a second the floor was a sheet of flame and he was burning. It happens so fast, fire does. You don't have a chance with it. Human beings are so—"

"Vulnerable." Dave looked at the other Wolfe books. They had the "A" too. 1935. Three years afterward the big writer had shared his pint of rye with a sick man on the Victoria-to-Vancouver steamer and caught the virus that killed him at thirty-eight. Eleven years younger than John Oats was when he died. "And it took a long time to patch him up. And you were around all the while, sold your house and your car to pay the bills." He turned and she was a blur because that was what the reading glasses made of everything distant. He took them off, folded the bows with a click, tucked them away. "He had life insurance. Didn't he have any other kind?"

She shut her eyes and gave her head a quick shake. "Only the usual automobile things. No health insurance. I mean"—her hands lifted and dropped—"he was so young, thought so young, moved so young. His body wasn't a man's nearly fifty. It was trim and hard, you know? Just naturally. He wasn't an exercise addict, he never dieted. Maybe if he'd had that kind of mind he'd have had Blue Cross or something. He didn't. He took his body for granted. It never occurred to him anything could go wrong with it because nothing ever had. It had always worked for him, it always would."

"Till it stopped completely," Dave said. "Life insurance he did have. And more than average."

"That was for others," she said. "Look, it wasn't just my house and car. It was his too, and the business, the bookstore, his part of it. Charles Norwood bought him out, his partner. It was everything. Even Eve. That was worst. While he was getting ahead, succeeding, she stuck with him. But when this happened and the doctors said he could die and that even if he didn't he probably couldn't lead a useful life again, she divorced him."

"Nice woman," Dave said.

"You can understand why Peter wanted out, then?"

"I can understand. And why he came here. You're special, Miss Stannard."

"Is that a way of saying 'crazy'?" she wondered. "Most people think I am—Mother's friends, the people down here in Arena Blanca, the doctors. What did I want with a man half eaten away by fire? Well, he wasn't 'a man.' He was John Oats. And I loved him. Before it happened and afterward and forever." Tears drew silver lines down her face. She smeared them with thin girl fingers, the nails short and without enamel. "I'm sorry."

"Did something happen to Peter's love?"

"I don't think so, no. He was going through changes. You do at that age. He was different from when he'd come down last summer. But not toward John. They were still good together. Warm and easy and funny with each other. But Peter was away a lot. At the Stage, the little theater. Acting was new with him. Books had been pretty much it till then. And his guitar. Now it was all acting. John and I went to the last play. A costume thing. Peter was very good. Natural. Mr. Whittington said afterward he had a great future if he'd keep working."

3

THE WATERWHEEL WAS twice a man's height, wider than a man's two stretched arms. The timbers, braced and bolted with rusty iron, were heavy, hand-hewn, swollen with a century of wet. Moss bearded the paddles, which dripped as they rose. The sounds were good. Wooden stutter like children running down a hall at the end of school. Grudging axle thud like the heartbeat of a strong old man.

A wooden footbridge crossed below the wheel. The quick stream under it looked cold. The drops hitting it played a chilly tune. The base of the mill wall next to the stream was slimy green with lichen. Higher, it showed rough brick. The building was tall, massive, blind as a fort. Old eucalyptus towered around it, peeling tattered brown bark, their shadows ragged blue on the whitewashed walls. A barn door fronted the mill. Posters were tacked to it, photos curling off them, actors' smiles bright, scowls deep. A smaller door had been carpentered into the big one, top and bottom halves separately hinged, a box-stall door. Above it, gold letters flaked off a crackled black signboard—EL MOLINO STAGE. Churchly. A bent finger of black iron poked through a slot in the door. He rattled it up and walked in.

The lobby was chilly and dim. Three steps from the door a long table on spindly aluminum legs trailed a white paper cover stained with coffee. A big coffeemaker stood on it, thumb-smeared chrome like the napkin dispensers, the screw tops of sugar jars. Polyethylene tubes that had held Styrofoam cups lay crumpled like ghosts of sleeves. Cigarette butts, ticket stubs, playbills strewed the plank floor. The high false wall of white plasterboard back of the table had a poster too, and photographs. The boy in the one labeled PETER OATS had the face of a young Spanish Christ.

Dave went through a doorway in the false wall and in the dark his shoe nudged steps quieted with carpet. He climbed them and stood behind ranks of wooden theater seats, six or eight shadowy rows. Matching rows went off at right angles to these. They framed on three sides an empty oblong of flooring over which, in deep reaches of gloom, boxy black spotlights clutched splintery rafters like tin owls. At the far end of the floor space daylight leaked around the edges of a black partition.

Beyond it he found a half-open door and beyond the door a big room with two high, narrow windows. Down one side of the room racks of iron gaspipe held costumes, glinting gold braid, shimmering satin, plummy velvet. The rest of the room was booths, two-by-fours and fiberboard, head-high. Empty coat-hangers dangled off the partitions. Bentwood chairs faced pine counters littered with wadded Kleenex, spent greasepaint tubes, empty soft-drink cans, under squares of cheap mirror, lightbulbed on either side, flecked with powder.

In a rear corner doors tagged MEN and WOMEN hung half open on darkness. A faucet dripped. In the other corner an iron staircase spiraled up. Its cleated treads gonged under his shoes. At the top he rapped a black door. Nobody came. He turned the knob, pushed, and the door opened. He wasn't sure what he'd expected—an office, a storeroom? It was a little of both, but it was also an apartment. Thick whitewashed walls and canted ceilings with charred beams. Dormer windows, small. Furniture from a dozen different periods.

"Hello?" he said. "Anybody here?"

No answer. The rugs were two and three deep, so there was no way to move but silently. He ducked the beams in the small dining space. A lot of copper hung against the mill's original brick in the kitchen. No sign or smell of meals past or to come. The pitch of the ceiling, the low beams were a real hazard in the bedroom. The bed was no place to sit up quickly. But the naked youth in the bed didn't show any sign of sitting up quickly. He lay on his front with a rumpled sheet tangled between his legs and breathed out stale fumes of alcohol. One hand hung off the bed edge. On the floor under it an eight-by-ten picture frame lay on its face. Dave picked it up, turned it over—carved wood brushed with gilt. There was no picture in it, only the glass and the cardboard backing. He frowned at the sleeping boy. He was dark, but his face was turned away. Dave wanted to see the face. He reached to touch the boy's shoulder and heard feet on the iron staircase. He set the picture frame on the bedside stand and left the room.

The knob of the black door rattled and a fat man pushed in, clutching brown paper sacks loaded with groceries. He must have weighed close to three hundred pounds. He was fair and blue-eyed. Pale reddish hair lay thin across his pink scalp. He puffed a little and turned to nudge the door shut. He had a musical voice. It almost tinkled. "Here we are. Food at last. Rise and shine. The shower head is a little tricky. If you—" He didn't finish the instructions. He saw Dave. The tinkling stopped, as if a screwdriver had been jammed into a music box. He tried to look outraged. He only managed to look scared. "Who are you? What do you mean—?"

"Is your name Whittington?"

"I think I'm the one to ask the questions." His eyes kept swiveling to the bedroom door. Sweat broke out on his upper lip, his forehead. "This is my home. I'm not accustomed to—"

"The place is public," Dave said, "a theater, a community-theater. The doors weren't locked. I walked through them. I'm looking for Pete Oats." He jerked his head toward the bedroom. "Is that Peter Oats?"

"Certainly not. That's my nephew. He's in the service. On leave. He spent the night," Whittington edged haughtily past Dave and up the short steps to the eating area. He waltzed, dodging the beams, got to the kitchen and set the stacks down with an annoyed tin-can clatter. "Not that it's any conceivable business of yours."

"It's my business." Dave went after him. Not carefully enough. He banged his head. He stood rubbing the bruise for a minute, then leaned in the kitchen doorway and watched the fat man empty the sacks and stow his haul away in cupboards and refrigerator. "Peter Oats's father drowned last week. His life was insured by the company I work for, Medallion. Peter was his beneficiary. The young woman where he used to live doesn't know where he's gone. I thought you might know. She said he used to spend a lot of time here."

"'Used to?'" Whittington's laugh was unamused. "Yes. She's right there. Lots of time. But not anymore." He cracked eggs into a mixing bowl as if they were hateful little skulls. "Now, if you don't mind—" He bent to flap open shutter doors under the sink. A wastebasket was alone there like a dwarf prince in a dungeon—royal-purple plastic embossed with gold fleur-de-lis.

Whittington winced and the hand with the eggshells hesitated a second as if it pained him to put the elegant thing to use. Then with a little twitch of his mouth he chucked in the shells and shut the doors. "I have breakfast to prepare, that boy to get fed, bathed, shaved, dressed and in his right mind. I have to drive him to the bus station in town and be back up here for a rehearsal at one. I haven't a minute to spare. If I had, I couldn't tell you a single useful thing."

"Peter Oats was pretty deep into theater." Dave lit a cigarette. "What suddenly turned him off it?"

With the sharp point of a paring knife Whittington slit the cellophane on a block of yellow cheese. He dropped the knife back into its drawer, found a grater and rubbed the cheese against it over the bowl that held the eggs. "You're utterly insensitive, aren't you?"

"I've got a job to do," Dave said.

"Peter got a swollen head, if you must know."

"How?" Four latticy white iron chairs stood at a latticy white iron table with a glass top at the near end of the room. A rococo pair of white plaster candelabra on the table sheltered a white fluted plaster urn full of fake peaches, apples, walnuts, autumn leaves. A big bivalve shell was there too, its pearly lining sooty. Dave tapped ashes into it and drew out a chair and sat on it. "I had the idea he was a nice kid, unspoiled."

"So had I." Whittington rewrapped the cheese and put it back in the refrigerator. "El Molino Stage has a reputation." He blasted the grater with hot water at the sink and stood it on the counter to drain dry. "As a result, people from Hollywood—the television companies, the film studios, the talent agencies—come here shopping for new material. A situation I deplore. But they pay for their seats. There's no way to keep them out."

"And one of them bought Peter Oats?" Dave asked.

Out of pink butcher paper Whittington spilled a string of little pink sausages into an iron skillet. He cut butter into another. He twisted burner knobs and circles of blue flame drew themselves under the pans. "Excuse me," he said and went out of the kitchen.

Dave heard him clap hands briskly and scatter words like merry bells around the bedroom. He got off the chair and crouched to open the shutter doors under the sink. The wastebasket held color transparencies, dozens of them, in tidy white cardboard frames. He lifted one into the steep slant of light from the window over the sink. Peter

Oats, suntanned in swim trunks, at the tiller of a sailboat, grinning, hair blowing, blue water, blue sky. Another. Peter Oats startled by a flashbulb at a ginghamed café table, fork half raised to half-open mouth. A third, Peter Oats in Renaissance tights, short velvet jacket, slashed puff sleeves, sword half drawn, snarling. Then the floor creaked where Whittington waltzed among the rafters and there was no more time. Dave dropped the slides, shut the doors and was standing staring out the bright window when the fat man came in.

"I should have known better than to star Peter in *Lorenzaccio*, but he was simply so right for it I couldn't resist, inexperienced as he was. I got my comeuppance. He was seen by, of all people, Wade Cochran."

Dave turned, squinting disbelief. "The Sky Pilot?"

Whittington nodded sourly. "Television's sagebrush saint. He was here night after night. Ostensibly to assess my abilities. But one night, very late, I heard a sound downstairs and found Peter, who'd come back for something he'd forgotten—his watch, I think. When he left, it was in Cochran's car. Not a car you'd confuse with any other—a bright yellow Lotus."

"Maybe he'd offered Peter a contract."

"I wasn't told and I wasn't about to ask."

"What would be wrong about that? What do you want for your people?"

"Theater. Television is to theater"—Whittington forked over the sizzling sausages—"what a billboard is to a Cézanne landscape. No, I think what happened to Peter, if indeed it did happen, is tragic."

"But do you know where he is?" Dave said.

The fat man dropped slices of bread into a toaster that swallowed them with a growl, like a shiny animal. "I do not know where he is."

"You mean he didn't stick with Cochran?"

"I mean people like Cochran are monotonously predictable. They lure innocent youngsters with promises they have no intention of keeping. They use them and discard them."

"Cochran's image is different," Dave said. "He's supposed to be as wholesome as he looks, as the part he plays. Lives with his old mother, always does what she tells him. Devout churchgoer, no smoking, no drinking. The morals good people held to when the West was young. Bible Belt."

"Tooled, no doubt," Whittington said.

And the boy came into the kitchen, the boy from the bed under the hazardous black beams. He was still naked and he was holding the empty picture frame. He did look like Peter Oats except without the trim edge of beard along the jawline. Also there was nothing saintly in his brown eyes. There was almost nothing at all. His handsome mouth asked Whittington:

"Whose picture was it? You said you'd tell me."

"Take your shower," Whittington said. "Breakfast will be ruined if you don't hurry. Leave the spray head alone or all you'll get is a totally unmanageable gush."

"Was he your lover?" the boy asked. Then he saw Dave and lowered the frame to cover his crotch.

"His name was Peter Oats," Dave said. "He used to act here."

"Act?" The boy looked blank.

"This is a theater," Dave said.

"Is it?" The boy's smile apologized. "It was kind of late when we got here. And I was pretty juiced." He frowned, tilted his head, blinked at Dave. "Are you a homosexual too?"

Whittington roared: "Take. Your. Shower."

"Sure. Okay. Sorry." The boy fled.

Whittington glared at Dave. "You know nothing about that picture."

"I know you threw out a good many others you had of Peter Oats." With his heel Dave nudged the shutters under the sink. "Which supplies the answer to the boy's question. He was your lover."

Whittington went red in the face. "For your information, Peter Oats is as straight as the proverbial stick. Now, I've asked you politely to get out and it hasn't worked. Shall I order you? Or"—he bunched muscles the fat didn't hide—"shall I throw you out?"

He had the weight. Dave went.

4

THE RANCH HAD a small valley to itself in rock-strewn hills
five miles back from the coast highway. The herd was token,
maybe twenty head, breeding stock, broad-backed, slab-
sided, short-legged, rust and white. They browsed on grass
that looked too green to be real. Horses moved in a rail-
fenced paddock, half a dozen palominos, coats glossy in
the winter sun. Beyond them, a framework of overhead
sprinkler pipes glass-beaded the shiny leafage of an orange
grove. Stable, outbuildings, the ranch house itself looked
like a movie set—plain, bat-and-board-sided, low-roofed,
sheltered by old oaks, red geraniums in window boxes.

The yard was flagged and cars stood there, a wide new
Chrysler station wagon, a black Lincoln limousine that
looked as if it got a lot of polishing but was filmed with
country dust now. And a yellow Lotus, looking like what
it was, a lethal toy. When he left his own car, a red setter
got up lank off the green-painted boards of the long, one-
step-up gallery of the ranch house and stood looking at
him. A bitch with pups somewhere. He walked to her, spoke,
bent and held out the back of his hand to her. She touched
it with a cold nose and her tail swung amiably. He scratched
her ears.

A string of varnished gourds, peppers, squashes hung gaudy next to the front door. Below it was a bell push. He thumbed it and inside chimes played four notes of a tune he hadn't heard since World War II. A gospel tune, "Love Lifted Me." He remembered a bleak barracks and the lonesome wheeze of a dollar harmonica. Then suddenly everybody singing. Everybody but him. He hadn't known the words. But he'd learned them. There was no way not to. Also obscene variations. He grinned to himself and a bony, freckled girl in a starchy green shirt-maker dress opened the door. No makeup. Frizzy red hair yanked back and knotted. Pencil stuck in the knot. Horn-rim glasses. In a forties movie she'd have turned out lovely in the last reel.

"Yes?" she said crisply. "May I help you?"

"I'd like to see Mr. Wade Cochran."

Her smile was weary. "So would several million other people. How did you find this place?"

"It took some telephoning. About an hour's worth. By me and a team of secretaries in my office. Screen Actors' Guild, American Federation of Television and Radio Artists, two agents, a business manager, a television studio, a recording studio, three police departments, sheriffs' offices in two counties, the state highway patrol, the bureau of records in Sacramento, the U.S. Department of Agriculture, the Cattle Breeders Association and I'm sure I've left out a few. I think I deserve to be rewarded for sheer persistence."

She wasn't amused. "Have you a card?"

He gave her a card and she read it and said, "But you telephoned. I told you he couldn't see you."

"Your error," Dave said. "You should have told me he was out."

"Mr. Cochran doesn't permit us to lie." She half shut the door, then opened it again, said, "Will you wait, please?" and closed it. Tight.

He crouched beside the setter, whose muzzle lay between her long front paws on the green boards. He scratched her ears again and she shut her eyes and rumbled contentment.

His look strayed to the empty hills. Not empty. A lone horseman rode the ridge at a walk. High above him a red-tailed hawk drifted on a lazy wind, sun haloing its wings. Behind Dave the door opened and the red-haired girl's voice said:

"Come in, please."

The set decorator had been here. The room was 1880. Pinks and bachelor buttons in the wallpaper. Furniture machine-carved walnut and oak glowingly refinished, upholstered in tufted black leather. Coal-oil lamps on marble-top tables with red ball-fringe throws. The girl led him across a floor of gleaming pine planks and braided oval rugs. Briskly. So he only glimpsed by the field-stone fireplace at the room's end a white-haired woman in dark glasses, seated in a wheelchair. Gaunt, big-boned, leathery. Mrs. Pioneer. A man with a mane of straw-color hair and a face like a new plow blade bent toward her from a platform rocker, talking. Mr. Evangelist. The red-haired girl opened double doors with narrow panels of fernleaf-patterned frosted glass. And it was the last half of the twentieth century again. A big swimming pool glittered blue in a flagged patio walled in by ells of the house. A swimmer angled toward the bottom of the pool. Dave's heart jarred. A man lay down there on his face, a clothed man, inert, limbs stirred by the motion of the water. The swimmer reached him, slid an arm under his chin, pushed backward and up, kicking for the surface, following the bubbles of his spent breath. He broke the surface, gulped air, shook back blonde hair and, still gripping the throat of the limp man in the crook of a muscular arm, half turned and with his free hand stroked for the pool edge.

When he reached it he grimaced, struggling to lift the unconscious weight. Dave ran to help him, crouched, gripped the body under the soggy arms and heaved upward. He staggered backward and nearly fell. Because it wasn't heavy. It had almost no weight at all. For seconds he stood there stupidly clutching it while its wetness soaked into his clothes. It wore a plain flannel shirt and Levi's and cowboy boots, but it wasn't a man. It was a dummy. He heard a chuckle. The swimmer grinned at him. In two easy motions he was out of the pool. "Thanks," he said. "But he's as near resuscitated as he's ever going to get. You don't need to bother with him anymore. Just let him down easy." He picked up a towel from a redwood chaise and dried his hair.

"What's the idea?" Dave asked.

"Next script I film"—there was a terry-cloth robe on the chaise; he flapped into it—"I got to rescue the boy in the story from drowning in a river." He knotted the sash. "It won't be easy as this, but I'm trying to keep the current and all that in mind." His grin made handsome gouges in his face. "That's where the acting comes in."

"Like the struggling you did just now to wrestle him out of the pool?"

"Like that. They'll have to weight him more in the river. But he'll never be more than fifty–sixty pounds, I expect." The accent was modified Southwest. Nothing else was modified. He stood six feet four and perfect. There were probably more beautiful men alive. Dave hadn't seen them. The actor stuck out a hand. "I'm Wade Cochran. You're Brandstetter. Katy tells me you went to a lot of trouble to track me down. What can I do for you?"

"I'm looking for someone. A boy. His father drowned last week. He was insured by my company. The boy is the beneficiary. His name is Pete Oats."

Cochran looked blank. "I don't know him."

"He was seen in your car late one night at the theater, the old mill, up the canyon back of El Molino. Remember? He had the lead in a play called *Lorenzaccio*. You were in the audience every night."

"Ah!" Cochran slapped his forehead. "That kid. Of course. Sure." He looked past Dave, who turned. The red-haired girl still stood at the end of the pool beside a black cluster of video tape equipment. Cochran called to her, "Katy, will you bring us out some of that cranberry juice?"

She walked brisk and prim along the far edge of the pool and vanished into a breezeway. A door closed.

Cochran said, "I drove him back to the theater one night. We'd been to a seafood place down in town there. Las Gaviotas. He'd been begging to talk to me." Cochran sat on the chaise. A redwood table was next to it, where an open shooting script lay. Then there was a chair. He tilted his head at it. Dave sat. "People pester you. But he had talent and I like to be fair." The far door closed again and he turned to watch Katy bringing a fat glass jug of red liquid and tumblers with ice cubes on a tray of Mexican hammered tin. She set it on the table.

"Will you be going to the lodge tonight?"

"I was. Who wants to know?"

"Your mother." Katy unscrewed the cap on the jug and filled the glasses. "She'd like the Reverend to stay over. He will if you're going to be here."

"All right," Cochran said. "I won't go till after supper and I'll be back to have breakfast with him. You can tell her."

Katy twisted the cap back on the jug. "She'd rather you stayed over. She's told the network people. They want to get footage of you here together. Tonight."

Cochran's mouth tightened. He wasn't happy, but he said, "Okay. If it's all right with the Reverend."

Katy smiled. "Oh, she's already arranged it with him. Thank you. She'll be so pleased." She went away.

"While we were eating," Cochran said to Dave, "the kid missed his watch. He was afraid to leave it up there, afraid somebody'd take it. 'Rip it off' is the way he put it. He didn't have a car. It's too far to walk. I drove him back."

"After the play closed, he stayed away from the theater," Dave said. "Whittington, the man who runs it, has the impression you made him some kind of offer."

Cochran shook his head and gulped from his glass. "You couldn't cast him in the stuff we shoot. He's too slight. Speech is too good. I don't expect to find anybody at that place—not for Westerns." He nodded at Dave's glass. "Try that. It's good stuff. Healthy. They say you drink enough cranberry juice, you'll never get cancer."

Dave tasted it and wondered how much would be enough. "Very good," he said. "Thanks. Why did you keep going back? Why did you stop after Peter Oats stopped? Why did he leave home about that time and not tell anyone—anyone living—where he was going?"

Cochran shrugged. "You're asking the wrong man."

Dave gave him a cold smile. "Not about why you kept going back to the play."

"I'm planning a feature on the life of Saint Paul. People said Whittington's a genius. You know, he was very big on Broadway, but when they started doing nothing but junk on Broadway he left. He made a couple films. Quit for the same reason. He's got integrity. I don't want some Hollywood hack. Those people are all corrupt. The director I hire's got to have brains and taste."

"And reverence?" Dave said.

"My team and I will supply that." Cochran swallowed more juice. "Anyway, I heard about Whittington and I went to size him up for myself. He was as good as they say, but I wasn't about to make a snap decision. This will take a couple million dollars, this picture, most of it my own. I'm walking around it a lot."

"Did you ask him? Will he do it?"

"I asked him," Cochran said. "He won't."

" He doesn't like the mass media," Dave said.

Cochran nodded. "Rather starve in that backwater, doing what he wants, what he thinks is important. Man can't help but admire that."

"He looks as if he gets enough to eat," Dave said.

"He's draining all his savings into that place," Cochran said. "My manager made inquiries. The city cut his budget this year. It wasn't but a few thousand to start with. Now it's nickels and dimes." He breathed a short laugh. "Know why he sent you here? Nuisance value. I gave him a check and he didn't like that. Oh, he kept it, but he hated me for being able to give it."

Dave said, "And you don't know what happened to Peter Oats?"

"Kids take things hard. Maybe after I turned him down he decided acting was no use. Maybe he was ashamed of failing and that's why he ran off. Didn't want to hear 'I told you so' from his folks. Lots of parents discourage their kids from acting. I thanked the blessed Lord every day for giving me the mother He did." Again Cochran looked past Dave. Again Dave turned.

The double doors with the frond pattern stood wide. The white-haired woman sat there in her wheelchair, the evangelist standing behind her. "Can't you quit and get in here now?" The way she turned her face toward where he wasn't told Dave she was blind. But she had a voice to holler up field hands against a prairie wind. "The Reverend will think I never taught you manners."

"Be right there." Cochran got up from the chaise. "Sorry I can't help. I expect when he gets over his bruises he'll turn up. You hang on to that money for him."

Dave rose. "It may not be payable."

Cochran blinked. "What's that mean?" Dave told him what it meant.

"No." Cochran scowled. "No, you don't know him. He couldn't. Why, he's as gentle as—"

"With twenty thousand dollars," Dave said, "he might not need a lot of help with his career." He held out his hand and Cochran shook it. Reflexively, still scowling, troubled. Dave told him, "Your girl Katy has my telephone number. Let me know if he should happen to get in touch with you."

"Sure." Cochran was unsmiling. "But he won't."

Dave scratched the setter's ears again on the porch. A horseman rode in at the yard gate. The same rider he'd seen on the ridge. Slight. Dark. But when he neared, he turned out to be forty, the skin on his bony face brown and creased as old harness. Not Peter Oats.

5

Ovals of leather patched the elbows of Charles Norwood's jacket. It was rugged Scots tweed and had been expensive some time ago. Soft gray fuzz sprouted on the back of his neck above a shirt collar that was frayed. A hinge screw of his glasses had been replaced by a snipped-off pin or paperclip. But his moustache was neatly trimmed, his shave was clean and close, his hands, straightening books already straight on a table marked Reduced, were well kept. His speech was modulated, the voice deep but a little old-maidish. His smile regretted.

"Peter? He hasn't been in here for months." Here meant Oats & Norwood: Antiquarian Books, in one of those arcades of shops favored in El Molino. Tall wrought-iron gates standing open in a thick archway to a courtyard paved with terra-cotta squares and enclosed by buildings of rough white stucco with roofs of curved red tile. Olive trees, dusty green and gray. A fountain weeping into algaed water from beneath the sandaled feet of a stained cement Saint Francis blessing stained cement doves. Real doves grieved overhead. The noise of late-afternoon street traffic was muted.

The shop was dim and hushed. But it probably was dim and hushed at high noon too. Its centerpiece was a big eighteenth-century globe of the world, rich with mottled greens and browns, cradled in a curved rack of time-mellowed wood. Dave spun it idly on its brass axis. His fingers came away dusty. "Since his father burned himself?"

Norwood nodded. "He left home about that time. Went to live with a girl in Arena Blanca. The same girl John went to after his discharge from the hospital."

"You know her name. She worked here."

Norwood smiled chagrin. "April Stannard. I've made a habit of avoiding it."

"For whose sake? I get the impression she was the only one, aside from Peter, who gave a damn for him. His wife walked out."

"Is that the way April tells it?"

"It's what she told me. Isn't it true?"

Norwood didn't answer. His hands stopped fidgeting with the books and he shifted his eyes. To a woman who stopped in the doorway. Dark glasses, blonde wig, fringed leather bolero over a white turtleneck jersey, fringed leather shoulder-strap purse at the hip of her white slacks. "Eve," Norwood said. "This man is from the company that insured John's life. He's looking for Peter."

The light was behind her. Dave couldn't see her expression, but she went very still for a second. Then she came to him in squeaky straw sandals with flat heels that clacked. She stood close, took off the dark glasses, frowned. She was very blonde. But time hadn't done her creamy skin any kindness. It was webbed like a winter-morning window in snow country. She was tall for a woman and looked strong, not heavy but strong. "Why Peter?" she said. "I was John's beneficiary."

"I'm afraid not, Mrs. Oats. He must have made a change when the two of you separated."

"But—" She didn't go on. She shut her mouth hard, turned abruptly and went fast through a doorway in a wall of books at the rear of the shop. Norwood drew a sharp breath. He started to reach after her. He didn't call out. He dropped the hand. He looked sick. As he stared at Dave, the corner of his mouth twitched. His voice came out a croak.

"There must be some mistake." He almost ran for a counter where a telephone squatted by a beautiful old cash register of pierced cast iron. "I'll call." He snatched up the receiver. "What's the number there?"

Dave's watch read 5:25. "The switchboard will be closed," he said. "But there's no mistake." He laid a card on the counter. "Call tomorrow. They'll tell you."

Numbly Norwood lowered the phone into place. In the room beyond the wall of books there was a quiet light now and a bottleneck rattled against a glass. Norwood heard it too. A dry tongue touched his lips. He gave a painted smile. "Well, I suppose you must be right. It's just such a shock. I apologize for getting excited." He flicked a glance at the door to the back room. In shadow above it, ghostly pale, a bust of Antinous bowed its head. "Look, would you excuse us now?"

"For drinks?" Dave said. "I'd even join you if you asked me."

Norwood jerked with surprise. "Why, I—" He smiled, stopped smiling, smiled again. "Of—of course. Pleasure. Eve?" He turned, rubbing nervous hands. "Mr"—he picked up the card and tilted his head back to read it through his bifocals—"Mr. Brandstetter will join us for martinis."

"Oh?" She stood in the doorway, a squat glass in each hand. The olives stirred, the ice cubes rattled. "Why?"

"I need to find Peter. Maybe you can tell me something that will give me a lead."

Her ice-blue eyes watched him for a quarter of a minute, then she gave a shrug and turned away. "I doubt it. But come in."

Under friendlier circumstances, *snug* would have been the word for the back room. Red leather armchairs faced a low golden-oak table where a Tiffany lamp glowed over books, catalogs, a loose stack of letters. The top letter looked like a booklist. He frowned. Where had he seen that elegantly engraved letterhead before? He shook his head. He couldn't remember.

On a desk under a window of wired frosted glass an old black L. C. Smith waited between stacked books stuck with slips of paper and a marbled pasteboard box of file cards. The desk was a bar too. Bottles glinted there. Shelves went darkly up all around, weighted by books and supplies. Eve Oats handed Dave a martini in a glass that matched hers and Norwood's but had a chip in its rim. Norwood, still looking pale, waved at a chair.

"Thanks." Dave sat and waited for them to sit. He looked at Eve. "Has Peter been to you? Did he come home?"

"What for?" She lit a cigarette. Her hands were unsteady. The match flame jittered. She shook it out and said flatly, "When he left home he took everything he owned." She blew smoke away as if it annoyed her, and swallowed a third of her drink. "He decided in his infant wisdom that I'd wronged his precious father and he hated me, couldn't live under the same roof with me another minute."

A sour smile tugged a corner of her mouth.

"'All right,' I said, 'go if you want to.' I think it shook him. He'd expected motherly tears and pleadings. The young live by cliché. But he went, grimly. No. I haven't seen him since." She took another long swallow of her drink. On the far side of the table the silent Norwood worked on his like an assignment. "I don't expect to. He was always stubborn. I'll never forget the fight he put up as a baby when the time came for him to begin eating solid food. Let me tell you"— her laugh was like crackling glass—"it was a contest of wills. I very nearly didn't win. He was determined to starve to death rather than eat that repulsive goop."

She finished off the drink and reached across the circle of light to collect Norwood's derelict ice cube. Her hand paused over Dave's drink. Her eyebrows queried. But he'd barely nicked it and he shook his head. She got up and rattled glass some more in the shadows around the desk. "I could tell you a boring succession of anecdotes about that child's mulishness."

"He was wrong about you and John Oats?"

"He had no understanding whatever of how things were." She came back and set Norwood's drink in front of him and dropped into her chair again. "He was far too young. They get the idea that because their arms and legs stretch and they're suddenly as tall as their parents, they're adults. Of course, he was wrong." She shook another cigarette from its hard pack. Marlboro.

"You didn't walk out on Peter's father when he was fighting for his life?"

The hand with the cigarette stopped on its way to her mouth. Her eyes narrowed and glinted dangerously.

"He's talked to April," Charles Norwood said.

"Ah. Has he." She didn't ask it, she said it. "Well"—she set the cigarette in her mouth, scratched a paper match and talked to Norwood—"I was going to tell him to go to hell with his prying." The match was curling back inside the flame. She touched the flame to her cigarette and dropped the match in the ashtray and leveled a hard look at Dave. "But I think I want to set the record straight. A short time after Miss April came to work here I found her with John in—shall we be elegant about it?—a compromising situation. In this very room. I understood. He was a man like all men. And like most men in their forties, foolish. She was very pretty, very young and, more importantly, very willing. That's understandable. John had a great deal of charm."

"She told me," Dave said.

"Yes, I'll bet she did. Well, I didn't make a scene. We talked it out sensibly, John and I, like grownups. John saw my point of view and April went. So that was that. Until his accident. Then she came back. To the hospital. I couldn't be there constantly. It takes at least two people to run this shop. She had no shop to look after. There's money in her background. The Stannards are an old El Molino family. She was there night and day, the nurses told me. John didn't know it. He was under heavy sedation. But there she sat, like something out of Olive Higgins Prouty."

Eve picked up her glass and tilted it steeply. This drink wasn't going to last even as long as number one. She set the glass down noisily. Her voice had the texture of a rusty file.

"Naturally when John began to be aware at all, it was faithful April he was aware of. I was a vague face that came and went. He didn't reason about it. Of course, a man in pain like that hasn't time for reason. I know it. But John was something of a special case. You see, Mr. Brandstetter—is that right?" She arched one brow. "The name?"

Dave said. "Yes, that's right."

"Scandinavian. Brand's daughter. Isn't that what it means? Yes. Funny." Her smile was thin and hungry. "You certainly don't look like anyone's daughter."

"Appearances can be deceiving," Dave said.

"Hah." She shot Norwood a dismal look. "Despite limited opportunities, I still know a man when I see one."

"John," Dave reminded her, "was a special case."

"Yes. He'd never been ill before. Never. He didn't know how to cope with it. Oh, life hadn't been exactly generous to him. He'd had disasters. But, you see, I'd always been there, right there, right at his side, to get him through somehow. He'd come to rely pretty heavily, pretty constantly on me for that. He'd make a mess, I'd pick up the pieces. Well, this was one mess I couldn't help with. No one could but doctors, nurses. And he couldn't grasp that. I'd always come to his rescue—for close to thirty years. This time I couldn't. I was as helpless as he was. And he hated me, really hated me for that." She drank again.

"April Stannard couldn't help him either."

"Oh, you are so right." Her mouth took a wry sad twist. "So completely right. But did he see it that way? No. Somehow her always being there made a difference." Her hands went up and fell like shot birds. "God knows what goes on in the romantic mind. I've never been able to fathom it. He said she 'loved him'"—Eve got rid of the phrase like bad food—"and I didn't. Good God! I ask you."

"Since it was all that could be done and she was doing it, maybe it was enough." Dave stood. "Can you give me some ideas about where Peter might be?"

"Your urgency puzzles me." She raised a hand to keep the lamplight out of her eyes and blinked up at him. "Insurance companies aren't known for frantic efforts to locate those they owe payments to."

"True. There's more to the story." He told it.

"Oh, seriously!" She laughed, shook her head, picked up her drink and finished it off. "I'm surprised at you. I'd thought you were complicated. How transparent. If he'd murdered his father, you wouldn't have to pay. It's not only transparent, it's sordid. And you didn't strike me as the least bit grubby. It shows how appearances deceive. I'm disappointed."

"Craziest thing I ever heard." Norwood got up and went with his glass into the desk dark. "Peter and his father were friends."

"Friends fall out," Dave said. "Mrs. Oats and her husband, for example."

"Ah," she said, "but John and I were never friends. We were dependents. He depended on me for common sense and backbone. I depended on him for—well, he was beautiful and charming. Draw your own conclusions." She bent into the light for her glass and held it out for Norwood. "But Peter and John might have been monozygotic twins. They thought alike, moved alike, spoke alike, looked alike. They cared for the same things. They were—I don't know the words for it—absolutely gone on each other, I suppose you'd say. They're the only two people I've ever known who lived together for twenty years and genuinely enjoyed every minute of it."

"And teamed up against you, I'm told," Dave said.

She got a new drink from Norwood. When she turned back, her smile was sardonic. "And were twice as weak that way. You see, they not only had each other's virtues, they had each other's flaws. It's what makes your fantasy so absurd. Neither of them would have had the courage to kill anyone." She frowned thoughtfully. "Except, of course, themselves. John was doing that. With morphine. It came out in the medical examiner's report at the inquest. He was an addict."

"It was for the pain," Dave said.

She shook her head. "The pain was long past. Ask Dr. De Kalb."

Norwood came back and sat down. "He could have drowned himself. He was badly scarred and he'd been proud of his looks. Also he had no money, no future."

"April didn't mind the scars," Dave said. "She was getting jobs. They were eating. There was a roof over their heads. April was his future."

"Peter," Eve Oats said stubbornly.

"Not at the end. His wanting to change the policy shows that. Peter had walked out on him. No, I don't know why. But they must have quarreled."

"Unthinkable." She held her hand against the light again. Its shadow masked her eyes. "Your eagerness to save your company money is muddling your mind. If Peter killed his father for his insurance, why hasn't he tried to collect it? What's he doing?"

"Having the horrors someplace," Dave said. "Murder takes some people that way. Doing it is one thing. Living with it is another. Thanks for the drink."

He went out through the dusky shop.

6

NIGHT MET HIM in the courtyard. He inched his sleeve back. 6:10. His mouth tightened. He ought to have phoned earlier. He had to phone now. Was there a booth? It waited in a dark corner like a child left over from a long-ago twilight game of hide-and-seek. It was an old wooden booth with wired glass and overgrown with ivy. When he stepped inside and unfolded the door shut to make the light turn on, tendrils of ivy groped through the hinge crack like roots into a coffin. A man wouldn't talk long here—not if he hoped to leave. He listened to the quarter rattle down. He dialed.

"*Allo.*" It had rung only once. That was bad. Behind the voice the stereo came through. Edith Piaf, Juliette Greco, Yves Montand? He couldn't make out. It didn't matter. He felt bad about them all. As he felt bad about the copies of *Paris-Match* that strewed the living room, as he felt bad about each new Genet letter in *The New Yorker*. For Doug they kept Jean-Paul alive, the smashed auto racer he had slept with, boy and man, during the two decades he'd worked for NATO in France. Dave's stomach muscles grabbed. He wanted to shout, *Turn it off!* He didn't shout. They never shouted at each other.

They weren't on that kind of footing. And maybe that was too bad. He said:

"That's the kitchen phone. You're cooking. So this call doesn't count. I'll be there."

"It's the bedroom phone. I'm not cooking. I just got out of the shower." Dave could see him, small, spare, palely naked—so like Rod, his own dead who wouldn't lie down—hunching a shoulder to hold the receiver while he scrubbed his shag of graying hair with one of Rod's red towels and dripped on Rod's white rug. "I've been at the shop since morning." He meant Sawyer's Pet Shop, kept by his bright, beaky little mother in one of those gray enclaves of neglect Los Angeles calls neighborhood business districts. "Emergency. The front of the big aquarium gave. We lost a lot of lives. Expensive ones. And I cut hell out of my hand. But the tank is fixed and I'm fixed. And there's *beaucoup* sand in the shower."

"Well, don't cook," Dave said. "I'm seventy-five miles away and I've still got a man to see here. Will you drive up? El Molino. There must be a good restaurant. I'll phone Madge. She'll know."

"Ask her to join you," Doug said. "She's closer. It's a hell of a drive from here, Dave, and it's the worst time of day for traffic." He didn't mind traffic. He lived to drive that red Ferrari of his and he drove it the way Szeryng played the violin. "And I'm tired, and my hand hurts."

"I'm sorry," Dave said. "Did you see a doctor?"

"Yes. It's elegantly stitched. It still hurts. I'll see you when you get here. All right?"

"Tomorrow," Dave said. "I'll phone you in the morning." He hung up. He hadn't known he was going to say that. Or had he? He felt hollow. Since last November, when they'd met at the sudden end of a policy-holder's heartbeats in a sand-flea beach-town rooming house, they hadn't slept apart. This would be the first night. Did he feel bad about that? If so, why? He waited a few seconds for an answer. It didn't come. But the hollowness didn't go. It began to hurt.

He fed the phone a dime and dialed Madge.

The place was called The Hound and Hawk. Thatch roof, white plaster, half-timbering outside, fume-oaked rafters and paneling inside. Leaded windows. Flamelight from logs in a huge fireplace glinted on the silver, crystal, white linen of still-vacant tables, and reflected ruddy in the polished broad-board floor he crossed to a short set of warped oak steps that climbed to a door marked TAPROOM. Torchlight, hanging rows of pewter mugs, taps bunged into oaken cask ends, a barmaid out of Holbein, frill-capped, buxom, rosy-cheeked. From somewhere a trickle of Morris Dance music, lute, hautboy, tabor. He hoped Madge would hurry. He had a low tolerance for sham.

He ordered Glenlivet with water on the side and put it away fast, dodging thoughts of Doug. And a second. And was working on a third when she stood beside him, tugging off driving gloves, unpegging her duffel coat, shaking back her wind-blown hair, boy-cropped, gray. He caught the tang of sea air when she hiked her long, fine bones on to the stool next to his. She gave him her good smile. It had been good for him for twenty-odd years. Dependable, real. He wished it was all he needed. He gave the smile back bleakly.

She pushed the gloves into a pocket, told the girl, "Margarita, thanks," and laid a lean, freckled hand on Dave's. "You look tired."

"Repeated encounters with nice, normal, everyday people who kill each other for money," he said, "can wear a man down after a couple of decades."

She winced for him. "Again? Who, this time?"

"A loving son, a not-so-loving wife, a pretty young mistress, a business partner"—he dug out cigarettes, lit one for her, one for himself—"or none of the above." His fingers turned the stubby glass in its circle of wet on the bar top. Blinking through smoke, he watched them. "If I knew, I'd leave word with the management here that they've got the wrong Elizabeth and go home."

"Home?" She cocked an eyebrow. "I thought you asked on the phone to stay over with me. You'd driven all over Southern California today and you were whipped."

The ashtray was thick pewter stamped with a coat of arms. Hound and hooded hawk. He tapped his cigarette on it.

She said, "I suppose you're aware that's never happened before."

He shrugged. "I'm not as young as I once was."

"It's not that. You'd have driven from Tierra del Fuego to get back to Rod at night. And it's not your work you're tired of, either. If you'll permit me an educated guess, it's Doug. Am I wrong?"

He drank and gave the flame-shadowed room a long, skeptical look. "I know you've never led me astray, but can the food here be really eaten?"

"Trust me." Her drink came, creamy, the rim of the stem glass frosty with salt. She tasted it, nodded approval, set it down with a delicate click and touched his hand again. "Talk about it, Davey."

He glanced at her and away. "*You* talk about it."

"Ah? Ready for an opinion now, are we?"

His laugh was short and wry. "You've had one prepared for some time."

"From the minute I met him. I thought I'd been masterfully deceptive about it. You knew?"

"That day at the raceway. The two of you with your heads together. The Ferrari owner, the Porsche owner. All that chat about Formula A versus Formula One, three liters versus five liters, V-eights versus flat twelves . . ."

New Year's it had been. Hard blue sky. Two-mile stretch of clean white grandstand. Flat black drag strip. Cars like toy-shop sharks, hammerheads. Crawling on squat tires. Then raw-throated engine roar. Track a jagged slash through new green landscaping. Along it McLarens, Lolas, BRMs screaming, snarling, skidding. For the inside, the front, the money. Average speed maybe ninety. Top speed maybe twice ninety. And off to the north, indifferent—brown mountains. Afterward, Doug, eyes shining, down in the clean concrete pit where the French team drank and laughed. Madge with him, very gay. Dave outside, above, hands jammed into car-coat pockets, shoulders hunched against wind that wrapped torn programs around his legs—watching, thoughtful.

"It was a little too real. Sure, you enjoyed it. But not that much. And not that way. You don't enjoy things that way. Doug didn't know, but I knew."

"Mmm." She had a mouthful of tequila, lemon, salt. She shook her head, swallowed. "No, no. You mustn't think I don't like him. I do. That makes it sadder."

"Than what?"

A hand touched his shoulder. He turned. A silver-haired man smiled deferentially. He wore a robe of brown velvet, ankle length, open down the front, gold-edged, with hanging sleeves. *Am an attendant lord*, Dave thought, *one that will do to swell a progress . . .*

"The dining room is beginning to fill, sir. May I reserve a table for you and the lady?"

"Thank you." Dave slid a bill from his wallet and folded it in the man's hand. "Not too near the fire, please. And can you leave us a menu?"

He did. It was folio size, the parchment cover stamped with the shield, the hound, the hawk, in crusty gilt. He dug out his reading glasses, let the bows fall open, slipped them on, opened the menu and turned it so the torchlight flickered on the lists. Crude black-letter type. Quaint spelling.

"No four-and-twenty blackbirds?" he wondered.

"Steak-and-kidney pie." Madge pointed it out. *Steke & Kydney Pye* was how the hired scholar had rendered it. "It's beyond belief."

"Like the rest of the place." Dave dropped the menu, clicked the glasses shut, pushed them away. "Hungry?" And when she nodded, he stubbed out his cigarette, laid bills on the bar, got down from his stool and handed Madge off hers. "Send another margarita to our table, please."

"Another Glenlivet for you, sir?" The barmaid's accent was Hollywood Cockney. "Thanks." He nodded and moved with Madge to the crooked steps again and down to where the firelight now had human faces to ruddy. The waiters were playing-card characters from *Alice in Wonderland*. Belted, open-sided tunics, green velvet, hound and hawk stitched in gold on the back. Yellow tights, a riband at the knee. Loose shirts with puffed white sleeves. They looked embarrassed. Dave wondered if their wives laughed at them. Their kids wouldn't—not kids these days. The problem would be to keep the kids from expropriating. Especially the slouchy yellow velveteen caps. Their waiter was missing his. Dave bet it was at a drive-in movie right now, a basketball game, a taco stand. After their drinks had arrived and he'd ordered and spoken to the cellarer— in a robe like the host's, only wine red, of course—he lit cigarettes for himself and Madge and asked her:

"Why did you wait till now?"

"Because you're the giver of wise counsel. Remember me? Twenty wrong choices in as many years. I never had anything but questions. You had answers."

"I've run out. I'm ready for yours."

"He looks like *Rod*. That was all there was to it. I was shocked you'd be so simple."

"He's a good human being. He's a grownup."

"That was always your formula for me." Her smile, her head-shake were rueful. "I never followed it."

"Until Sylvia." Miss Levy was plain and thirty-five, a college librarian, nothing like the handsome, coltish boy-girls Madge—a clever and successful designer, not of her life, but of textiles and wall-coverings—had pursued from one calamity to the next through a wreckage of years. None of them had been worth her time, certainly not her grief. Most had simply used her. It had pained Dave to witness. "How is Sylvia?"

"Wonderful." Madge glowed. "It was good advice, Davey, even if it did take two decades of disaster to make me accept it. I'm grateful."

He shrugged. "Other people's problems are easy."

"All right. Let me try at yours." She tasted the margarita, set it down, looked grave. "Yes, he's a good human being. Yes, he's a grownup. As are you. But when you found each other, you were both in deep trouble. Not used to loneliness. Not able to cope. You'd had Rod. All your adult life. He'd had Jean-Paul. He's shown me photographs of Jean-Paul." In magazines, newspapers, souvenir programs, French, English, Italian, yellowing at the edges. Dave knew them. In a cardboard carton in a closet. More than once he'd started to throw them out. Madge said, "He was underweight, with beautiful square shoulders. Like you." She reached across to brush the fall of straight hair off his forehead. He liked her touch, cool, dry. "Blond like you, blue-eyed." She took the hand back and her smile regretted. "It couldn't have been a sadder coincidence."

"People have to look like somebody," he said.

She frowned, picked up her glass, studied him across its circle of salt. "Why don't you want to go home and sleep with him tonight?"

"For the same reason he didn't want to come up here and have dinner with me."

She nodded, tasted the drink, set it down. "Because he can't be Rod. Because you can't be Jean-Paul."

"I guess we both figured it out about the same time." With a finger he turned the little block of ice in his glass and watched the straw-yellow whiskey curl around it. "Not very quick. Not very bright."

"You could try loving each other. Under your real identities. You're both worth loving."

"You've told me. Who's going to tell him?"

"You are. Tonight. When you get home."

"Home?" he said. "Where's that?"

7

A VERY SMALL girl opened the door. It was a heavy door and it took her backward with it a few steps before she remembered to let the knob go. Her yellow flannel sleepers were printed with drawings of the comic-strip dog Snoopy. A rubber band tugged her taffy hair into a topknot, but some strands had got away and were damp. She was rosy from scrubbing. She clutched a plastic duck.

"I had my bath," she said. "Now Daddy's going to read to me about snakes."

"That sounds like fun," Dave said.

Back of her, in a long sunken living room where gentle lamplight glowed on glossy new Mediterranean furniture, a pair of older children, six, eight, sat on deep gold wall-to-wall carpet and watched television. Winchesters crackled. Orange Indians tumbled from purple horses. A young woman came between him and the action. She wore splashed denims, but starchy white was what she was used to. She moved like a nurse. She was blonde as the child, her eyes were Delft blue like the child's—but not childish. Armed.

"Dr. De Kalb," Dave said.

"He doesn't see patients at home." One hand eased the child backward, the other began to close the door. "If you'll call the office tomorrow morning and make an appointment—"

"I'm not a patient. I'm from Medallion Life."

"Thank you." Her smile flicked on and flicked off. "We have all the insurance we need."

"The death-claims division," Dave said. "It's about a former patient of his. A man who drowned."

"Oh?" She frowned, but she stopped moving the door. She turned and spoke into the room. "Phil?"

The chair De Kalb unfolded from faced the television set, but he hadn't been watching. He'd been reading. The book was in his hand. Gray and heavy. A medical text. He kept a finger in it as he came to the door. He looked young, but he walked old, a stoop to his shoulders. He was tall and lanky, a towhead like his wife and kids. His eyes were Delft too but hidden under a bony thrust of brow. His ears stuck out. They didn't look adaptable to a stethoscope.

"Thanks," he told his wife, and she gave him a smile that was brief but real and led the little girl away, and he asked Dave, "What's the problem?"

Dave gave him a card. "It's about John Oats."

"Ah." De Kalb winced and shook his head. "That was tragic, damn it." He stepped back. "Come in."

The room he led Dave to was down steps and out of range of the television gunshots. Desk and coffee table were deal. Easy chair and couch were tawny corduroy. The walls were knotty pine and crowded with glittering sports trophies on wooden brackets, sports photographs in frames. A few were team pictures—baseball, basketball. But most were of De Kalb solo. Younger but unmistakable. Head thrown back, muscles strained like wires, face twisted in agony, chest snapping a track-meet tape. Leaping straight as an exclamation point to slam back a high drive on a tennis court, packed bleachers in the background. Jackknifed in mid-air over a tourney swimming pool. No wonder he walked old. He laid the book on the desk, dropped into the easy chair, nodded at the couch.

"I don't understand it," he said. "John was doing just fine. Considering the extent and severity of his burns, he'd come back very well. No sign of liver dysfunction, which is what you really fear in these cases. He was a happy man the last time I saw him. Why would he kill himself?"

"Did he?" Dave sat and lit a cigarette. "The coroner's jury called it accident."

"Hah. They never swam with him." De Kalb stretched a long arm, rattled open a drawer of the desk, brought out an ashtray. "Scars and all, he could outlast me."

It was a little glass square, the kind non-smokers keep. A red-and-black ad for an unpronounceable drug product was stenciled on its bottom. Dave set it on the couch arm. "Where?" he asked.

"Arena Blanca. He asked me there for drinks and dinner, Christmas week. After sundown, we swam. Before, we sailed. With a friend of Peter's. His boat? I don't know. Catboat, twenty- footer. Very pleasant. That's a pretty bay, sheltered by those hills. Calm."

"Do you remember the friend's name?"

"I wouldn't have, but I've run into him since. Jay McPhail. He works nights and weekends at the drugstore in that new shopping center. On the coast road. Not far from the turnoff to Arena Blanca. Yup. Some developer will make a packet off all that white sand and blue water, once the rich old widows who own those rickety places die off."

"One of them did. April Stannard's mother."

"Nice girl." De Kalb frowned. "That's another thing. Why would he kill himself when he had a lovely girl like that? She really cared about him. She was at that hospital—"

"Night and day," Dave said. "Eve Oats told me. She also told me to ask you if he was still in pain."

De Kalb stared. "Pain? Certainly not."

"Then why was he on morphine?"

De Kalb sat up sharply. "What?"

"You weren't at the inquest?"

"No. I was in New York. For a meeting of dermatologists." Bleak smile. "Also for the Indoor Track and Field Championships. Took off from LA International that same night. The night John died. Didn't know that then, not till I got back. But flying you remember the weather. And it was raining, yes, but you couldn't really call it a storm. No wind to speak of. The bay wouldn't have been rough."

"He was found on the rocks out at the point."

Headshake. "He wouldn't swim out there."

"That's what I think. All right. What about the morphine? Was he on it at the hospital?"

"Oh, yes, certainly. At first. It was indicated. But no longer than necessary. The danger of addiction isn't exactly news to us."

"And you took him off it?"

"When we could. Too soon for him. He begged. They often do, afraid the pain will come back. It won't. We don't start withdrawal until we know it won't. But there can be panic. That's not easy to face. It's one of those times you have to be ruthless. With them and with yourself."

"It was in his system when he died," Dave said. "There were the usual needle marks, lots of them. He never did get off it."

De Kalb made a grim sound and pushed up out of the chair. Hands shoved into pockets, he moved to a window. It was a black mirror. He glowered at his reflection without seeing it. "We change the dispensary locks. It doesn't help. Too many people have to have keys. Regulations are strict, but emergencies happen. Doors get left unlocked, keys fall into unauthorized hands." He turned back, a pallbearer slump to his shoulders. "And, as I expect you know, the drug-addiction rate among physicians is high. That makes it awkward for the nurse in charge when things turn up missing. The police most often don't get called. It's a mess. And it doesn't get better. It gets worse."

"No idea who gave it to John Oats?"

"Probably an orderly." De Kalb's sigh was harsh. He dropped loose-jointed into the chair. "They come and go. The work is hard, sometimes gruesome, the pay is poor. We've caught them in the past. They find out what patients are being withdrawn. It's a way of picking up an extra five, ten dollars."

"It would be a way of picking up a lot more than that after the patient was out of the hospital." De Kalb's head tilted. He blinked, puzzled.

"I mean, in the back of his mind the hospital patient who's an addict knows if he's caught he'll be taken off the stuff in easy stages. But once outside he's on his own. I understand abrupt withdrawal can be unpleasant."

"It starts with yawning that you can't control," De Kalb said. "Sometimes it breaks the jaw. Shivering that seems as if it will shake you to pieces. You sweat in a way you can't believe a human being could. If you're lucky, you sleep. After a fashion. But you wake up. And the mucus begins running. You think you'll drown in your own mucus. Some do. And you're cold and there's no way to get warm. Then the vomiting starts and the diarrhea. Your muscles go crazy. You try to cover yourself and get warm, but your legs keep kicking the blankets off. You get up and walk. If you've got the strength. It doesn't help. Nothing helps. You lie on the floor. And you scream."

"That should drive prices up," Dave said.

De Kalb's hands made big, knobby fists on the chair arms. "I'll get whoever did it."

Dave shook his head. "Get the police. Ask for Captain Campos. He bought the verdict on John Oats, but only because he's overworked and it saved time. This will turn him around. And he'll handle it well." Dave stood. "In my job I meet police officers. I'd take Campos for one of the bright ones."

De Kalb got up. "I'll call him in the morning."

"Doesn't that hospital have a night shift?" Dave asked. "Call him now. It was nine this morning when I saw him, but police hours are long. He may still be at work." A telephone in wood-grain plastic sat on the desk. Dave picked it up and held it out to him. "If not, call him at home. When he knows what it's about, he won't mind."

The little girl came down the carpeted stairs. Sideways. One step at a time. "Daddy, Daddy!" She was flapping an open book. Dave glimpsed a diamond-back rattler mottled among mottled leaves. "Read to me. Mommy says she doesn't like snakes." Tears were in the blue eyes. The pink mouth trembled. "And you promised, you promised."

De Kalb set down the phone and picked her up. "I promised," he told her, "and I will. Just as soon as I make one telephone call." He used a fingertip to wipe her tears away.

"I'll go," Dave said.

8

THE SHOPPING CENTER was a cry of light against the hulking darkness of the hills. Its signs were crisply lettered sheets of milky plastic, its shopfronts naked glass, the interiors ice-white fluorescent. Brave but lonely. Safeway, Laundromat, Kentucky Fried Chicken, liquor, Newberry's, hairdresser, drugs. Three cars waited on space enough for thirty. Dave left his pointed at the drugstore and pushed inside.

The silence was large, but a typewriter was snipping little holes in it. Slowly. At the rear. Dave went there between hedges of toothpaste, deodorants, laxatives. The counter was chin high and topped by old-fashioned glass urns filled with dried herbs, for cuteness, not use. The urns were labeled in Spencerian script. The sign overhead was Spencerian too, gold on a white oval: PRESCRIPTIONS. A boy looked at him between the urns. His tightly curled black hair was parted in the middle and combed over his ears. His brown eyes dreamed and his mouth was a dark rose. He could have posed for a Rossetti drawing. He could have been Rossetti, young, before the bloat set in.

"McPhail?" Dave said.

"McSucceed," the boy said. "At least till now. What's wrong?"

"Does something have to be wrong?"

"You didn't say Mr. McPhail, you didn't say Jay McPhail. You said McPhail. For some reason, that sounds official. And you look official. Did I mess up on a prescription?"

"You're a friend of Peter Oats. I'm looking for him. I'm from the company that insured his father's life. His father's dead. Peter was the beneficiary."

"Just a second." The typewriter tapped some more. The platen ratcheted. The boy came to the end of the counter where its height dropped and there was a coral-color cash register and a flat glass-top display box of razor blades and small flashlight batteries. His white jacket was open. Under it was a pirate-stripe skivvy shirt. His pants were bell-bottoms, tie-dyed purple. A little bottle sparkled in his hand. He licked the label he'd typed and pasted it to the bottle that held cotton and some red-and-gray capsules. "I haven't seen Peter for a while. I'm going on with school. He's not. He's into acting. Would you believe?"

"Would it be difficult?"

"It's far out, man. I mean, he's so quiet. He taught himself guitar, you know? He's got a good voice. Would he sing for anybody? Hell, no. He liked lonely things, climbing, riding, swimming. He doesn't look strong, but he is. Mostly he read, listened to records, classical music. Then, all of a sudden, he's acting. With Whittington and the rest of those fags."

"Is he a fag?" Dave said.

McPhail's Pre-Raphaelite eyes hardened. "I was his best friend all through EMSC. Do I look like a fag?"

"I don't know what a fag looks like," Dave said. "And neither does anyone else. You took him sailing Christmas week. With his father and Dr. De Kalb."

"In my folks' boat. That was the last time I saw him. Except around town with Whittington. Always with Whittington. Jesus!" He scrawled a name on an envelope that was printed with a yellow mortar and pestle, dropped the pill bottle into it, tucked it away under the counter. "Too bad about his father. I really grooved on him."

"Was it the last time you saw him too?"

The boy straightened, wary, turned his head, watched Dave from the corners of his eyes. "I said—"

"I heard what you said. But John Oats was on morphine. Morphine is a prescription drug."

"He didn't have any prescriptions. He bought shaving cream here. Tooth powder. That's all."

"Bought isn't what I'm talking about. You liked him. He was your best friend's father. Did you give him what he needed?"

"Shit!" The boy hit the release bar on the cash register with his fist. The drawer opened with a jingle. He slammed it shut. "Okay. I guess it can't hurt him now. No. I didn't give it to him. But he asked me. I found him in here one morning when I opened up. Poking around in the dark"— the boy jerked his head—"back there. He was in bad shape, sweating. He'd broken in. He wanted to steal it, but he couldn't find it. He begged me for it. Sad. Christ, how sad!"

"You didn't report it."

"He was Pete's father," the boy said. "He was a good man, a fine man. I wouldn't do it to him. How could I? Would you?"

"What did you do?"

"Offered to phone his doctor. De Kalb. He wouldn't let me. I couldn't make sense out of his reasons. I don't think they were reasons. He was just scared, sick, ashamed. I ended up driving him home. Nice of me, wasn't it?" Self-contempt soured the words.

"You know the answer to that," Dave said.

"No, I don't. Not what you mean. He's dead. Maybe it was because I didn't help him."

"Somebody helped him," Dave said. "If that's the term for it. Don't blame yourself."

"I couldn't make myself give it to him. If he got caught, it could be traced. I worked hard to get to be a pharmacist. And I'm working hard to get to be a doctor. I'd be finished. That was all I could think of. Me." His smile was miserable. "Makes me one of the good guys—right?"

"Did you tell Peter?"

"Christ, no. How could I tell Peter?"

"And you don't know where he's gone?"

"Sometimes when things got bad in his life—he and his mother didn't get along too well—he'd take a sleeping bag and drive off alone. It was bad, his father drowning. He really loved his father."

"So they tell me," Dave said.

He stepped out of the car into a wind that was cold and damp. He shivered, turning up his collar, and crunched across the sand to the pink house that was no color in the night. The warped garage door hadn't been pulled down. The old station wagon was still there, a pale hulk in its stall. He climbed the high flight of wooden steps and at the top felt for the corroded button and pushed it. The buzz came back too loud. He squinted, pawed for the door, touched space. Open.

And no one came. He lifted and tilted his wrist. His watch said greenly 9:50. Twelve hours since his first time here this morning. Had she tired herself out with housecleaning and gone to bed early? He poked the buzzer again. It echoed on emptiness. But then he heard footsteps below. Backed by the dark wash of night surf only a few yards off, her voice came thin.

"Peter? Is that you?" She set a quick foot on the steps. Dave felt the rickety framework shiver. "Sorry to be a disappointment twice."

She halted. Down where she was, a disk of light showed. Feeble but evidently strong enough to reach him. "Oh, it's Mr. Brandstetter." She didn't care. The light went out, but she didn't come up. He waited a second, then he went down. She was wearing a man's corduroy jacket, much too big for her, the cuffs clumsily turned back. John Oats's jacket? She turned away and her voice sounded as if she'd been crying. "I was walking on the beach when I saw your headlights. I thought it had to be Peter this time."

"I haven't found him. No one else ever comes?"

She shook her head, stepped down on to the sand, moved off. "No. And that was fine when John was here. It's not fine now."

He went with her down the softening slope of dimly white sand toward the black shift and whisper of the bay, its chill breathing. At its inmost curve the window lights of houses rippled yellow on the water. Shadow boats rocked asleep at shadow jetties. He said, "Dr. De Kalb came Christmas week. Jay McPhail."

"That was a good day," she said. "John was really pleased, really happy."

"But no one else? No one since?"

"Someone ate supper with him the night he—" But she couldn't say it. She walked more quickly, hunched inside the bulky coat. He lengthened his stride. She changed the wording. "That last night. But it must have been Peter. I told you—John's friends never came."

"What about strangers?"

She halted, turned. "I thought you wanted Peter. He killed his father—isn't that what you said? For the precious insurance money your company doesn't want to pay him. Now its strangers. Why?"

"John Oats used morphine. You heard that at the inquest. What you didn't hear was that he had no prescription. I checked that out with Dr. De Kalb tonight. And with Jay McPhail."

"At the drugstore? In the shopping center?"

"He found John Oats there early one morning. He'd broken in. He was looking for morphine. He begged Jay for it."

"No. Ah, no."

"He brought him back here. Where were you?"

"Driving to work, I suppose. I never knew him to leave here, not without me, without the car. It's such a long way."

"Farther than he thought."

"He never said a word to me. And I never saw—I mean, he didn't want me to look at him. Because of the scars.

It's the arms where they put the needle, isn't it? He kept them covered—long-sleeved shirts, pullovers, pajamas. I told you he swam at night. He always wore a robe down. And he wouldn't let us swim with him. Not me, not Peter. Dr. De Kalb that once, but that was different, he was a doctor." She drew a breath. "And when we—made love, it was always dark."

"In more ways than one," Dave said.

She shut her eyes and nodded. "Yes." She turned from him to stand, hands in the jacket pockets, wind fluttering her hair, staring. At what? Dave narrowed his eyes. Rocks. Thirty feet from shore, black and ragged in the starlight, edged by a dim embroidery of foam. The place where she'd found John Oats's body. "It hurts," she said. "You always bring pain with you."

"Who brought him the drug, Miss Stannard?"

"I don't know." She stared away silent for a minute longer. Then she turned to him, laid a light hand on his arm. Her eyes pleaded. "Come up to the house with me? Have a drink?"

"Thanks," he said, "but someone's expecting me."

It was the third station. Floodlit yellow metal, plate glass. A black boy in a yellow jumpsuit squatted on his heels, hosing down tarmac that was already immaculate. He used his thumb to make a stiff spray. It seemed important. But when Dave braked beside the shiny pumps he dropped the hose and came jogging, smiling.

"Whatever it will hold," Dave said, got out and watched him flap open the gas hatch, twist off the tank cap, shove the nozzle in. The pump hummed. Dave said, "A few nights back a girl driving an old Ford station wagon broke a fan belt along this road. Was it here she got a new one? It was raining. It was after nine."

The smile died. The brown eyes looked him up and down. Stonily. "If it was a new car, would you ask? If she was over thirty?"

Dave didn't answer. The boy turned his head to watch the numbers rolling up like martyrs' eyes behind the pump's glass. When they quit, he put everything back. Dave handed him a credit card. He took it to a yellow cashbox at the end of the row of pumps, wrote on a thick form pad, brought the pad for Dave to sign, gave him back his card, gave him his receipt and met his stare. He took a deep breath, held it, let it out. Not happily. "All right. I put it on for her, yeah. I hope it don't cost her twenty to life or something."

Dave shook his head. "Only what you charged her."

The station had a pay phone, encased in a blue plastic shell like an outsize crash helmet. He used it to phone Madge. To tell her he wasn't coming.

9

THE HOUSE WAS dark. He checked his watch. Not midnight yet. And the Ferrari was in its stall. Odd. He shut down the garage, used the service-porch door, stepped up, passed a hand over the small glow of a thermal wall switch and lit the kitchen. On the bricked-in burner deck a glass coffeemaker glinted half empty beside a big red-enameled cast-iron fry pan gummy with tomato sauce, a red-enameled cast-iron pot that had held wild rice. In the sinks lay carbon-steel knives, for chopping, for carving, big metal spoons. On the counter a pair of long wooden forks slept in a wooden bowl with scraps of lettuce, circles of onion. A gold can of olive oil, a thin-necked bottle of tarragon vinegar stood guard with a wooden pepper mill.

He swung toward the shutter doors into the dining space and noticed a square of paper Scotch-taped to the red wall phone. CAMPOS was lettered on it in felt pen, bold and quick, Doug's writing. Under the name was an El Molino number. He peeled it off the phone, tucked it in a pocket, pushed the doors. While they did their wooden butterfly imitation behind him, he lit the room. Two settings at the table. Tomato-stained plates crisscrossed by Danish flatware. Empty cups and glasses, empty wine bottle. A thicket of frail candles melted halfway down.

Had Doug brought his mother for dinner? His hand was bandaged, but it wouldn't be like Mrs. Sawyer not to wash up afterward.

A pass at another thermal switch brought circles of light from chrome Bauhaus lamps below in the living room. They gleamed on Parsons tables in high-gloss orange and blue, on long white couches strewn with color-swirled cushions, on a snow prairie of white carpet, a scatter of gaudy record covers in front of a turntable hooded by smoked Plexiglas. He went down the three wide steps. At the room's far end white shutter doors closed off a short hall, linen closet to the right, bathroom to the left, bedroom at the end. He started for the doors and stopped.

Over a couch arm lay a jacket, windbreaker type, glossy purple satin orlon. Frowning, he picked it up. Words were stitched across its back in pale lavender script: EUROPEAN MOTORS. He turned it around. In matching script but smaller, high and to the left of the zipper, was the name LORANT. Dave knew European Motors. It was where Doug had the Ferrari tuned. All the mechanics were born overseas, factory-trained overseas for work on foreign cars. Lorant wasn't French but, Dave supposed glumly, close enough to it—Belgian. He'd shaken hands with him at the garage. Lean, blond, blue-eyed. *With beautiful square shoulders.* Dave dropped the jacket. Turning off lights as he moved, he went back to the kitchen and dialed the number on the note.

In blue on a wrist no thicker than a ten-year-old's a tattoo needle had punctured the words BORN TO LOSE. Another kind of needle had punctured the chalky skin of the arm farther up. The boy kept rubbing the place. He sat in T-shirt, jockey shorts and fallen dime-store socks on a tan metal chair in an old room where tan paint was new on bare walls. On a tan metal table in front of him lay his coverall, green starched cotton, EL MOLINO HOSPITAL stitched in white on the breast pocket. With eyes the color of dirty water he stared across the table at Jesus-Maria Campos, who sat, and at Dave, who leaned in the doorway, smoking. He wasn't aware he was rubbing his arm.

"You got an infection there?" Campos asked.

"Fuck off," the boy said, and stopped rubbing.

"No—you wouldn't have." Campos was slim, even delicate. His hair was going. It lay across his scalp like black fishbones. He wore a Mexican *bandido* moustache and sideburns. His sand-color uniform was tailored and knife-edged, but it had been a long night and patches of sweat were dark on its back and under its arms. "You wouldn't get an infection— not using hospital needles."

"I sell my blood," the boy said, "to the Red Cross. Needles is how they get it."

"Once every three months." Campos shook his head. "Too many marks."

"I got small veins. And the nurses they got are all trainees. They keep jabbing around till they find the place."

"Yeah, and so do you." A paper lay in front of Campos. In its upper right corner were pasted two Polaroid photos of the boy, front face, profile, scared, sulky. Along the bottom margin, fingerprints were black in ruled boxes. Between the photos and the fingerprints, typing filled in blanks. Campos turned the paper over. Writing in blue ballpoint took up one and a half lines on the back. "After they brought you in and put you through the routine, a doctor saw you, remember? You pissed in a bottle for him. The lab ran a stat on that sample. It's called a naline test. Your urine showed opium derivatives. Morphine is an opium derivative. The dispensary at the hospital keeps missing morphine. In quantity."

"It puts you to sleep." The boy wanted to make friends with a clock over the door above Dave's head. His look kept going to it. It didn't seem to give him any satisfaction. "I'm not sleeping."

"You will be," Campos said, "but you'll hate it."

The boy's voice went shrill. "The dispensary! Everybody helps theirself at the dispensary. But you don't bust none of them. You bust me."

"'Born to lose,'" Campos said. "Right?"

"You better believe it. Plenty of doctors in that place are hypes. But if a doctor pissed in that bottle, your lab would tell you it was full of tropical fish."

"One law for the rich, one law for the poor?" Campos said. "I know about that. You grow up a Chicano in this town and you know about it. But if you want to change it, you're starting at the wrong end."

A tough brown nine-by-twelve envelope lay under the paper with the photos and fingerprints. Campos pried up its little tin clasp, opened its flap, upended it. A wallet fell out, plastic that had never even tried to imitate leather. A rattle of pennies, dimes, quarters. A limp matchbook, a crumpled Kent cigarette pack, a nail-clipper, a little loop of tarnished ball chain with three keys on it. Campos took one of the keys off and tossed it in his palm. It winked in the cold overhead light. The boy watched it as if it were the only object in the room. Pale, like something from under a stone, his tongue came out, touched his lips, went back into the dark again.

Campos said, "This is a key to the dispensary. You aren't supposed to have a key to the dispensary."

"You said 'in quantity'!" the boy shouted. "Even if I was a user, how could I use it in quantity?"

Campos let the key fall. "You could sell it."

The boy had come in sallow. Now he looked made out of cheap wax. "Jesus!" he whispered. "I wouldn't waste ten seconds on you"—Campos held open the brown envelope and dropped the wallet into it, the rest of the stuff, the keys—"if it was only yourself you were hurting."

"You're out of your skull," the boy said. "If I was a pusher, would I be swabbing up shit at that hospital all night? At a dollar-sixty-ass-five an hour?"

"It's your source." Campos fitted the hole in the envelope flap over the upright tin prongs and flattened them. "And your cover."

The boy laughed. There was despair in it. "You seen the dump I live in? You seen the car I drive? A beat-up '58 VW."

"It got you to Arena Blanca. To John Oats. Not once. Several times. Beginning when he left the hospital, back around Christmas."

"Who?" The boy squinted. "Arena what?"

Campos sighed. "Put on your coverall." He turned his head. Not far. He was too tired to turn it far. Just enough so Dave knew the words were meant for him. "Bring her in, will you?"

He found her in a room where vending machines, battered but flashy, stood against the walls like images left over from a religious procession. In a corner was a tan swing-top waste receptacle, but it was jammed and the floor was a trash map of candy wrappers, sandwich scraps, striped waxpaper cups. Arm desks of tan steel tubing and varnished plywood made a back-to-back row that divided the room. In the flat 2:00 A.M. glare of naked fluorescent ceiling lights, four people kept apart from each other at the desks. A bald black man leaned forward, big hands hanging, staring at his paint-stained shoes. Over the thick knees of a Mexican grandmother a frail brown little boy climbed, whining in Spanish to go home. April Stannard waited, pale, her girl hands knuckled together in her lap. When she saw Dave, she frowned and stood up. She wore a coat of her own now.

"You're here," she said. "So it's not good news."

"I don't know what kind of news it is. It may not be news at all. Captain Campos will fill you in."

She went with him down a hall that was a tunnel of echoes. The dying moan of a siren from outside. Jangle of a telephone nobody wanted to answer. A woman's voice, arguing, insistent. Chatter of teletype machines. Sudden male laughter. Campos waited outside the shut door of the small room. In one delicate hand he held the typed and fingerprinted sheet and the brown envelope. The other hand was on the doorknob. He gave April a smile too tired to last.

"Sorry to keep you waiting so long. I want you to look at somebody for me. He's in this room. When I open the door, don't say anything, please. All I want is for you to get a good look at him. Then we'll go to my office and talk about it. All right? Ready?"

April started to say something. About melodrama? She changed her mind and nodded. Campos twisted the knob, swung the door inward. The boy had put on the green coverall. It was too big for him. He stood, rubbing his arm again, staring out a window whose heavy steel mesh was clotted with years of repainting. At the sound of the door latch he turned. He saw April and his head gave a sick twist away.

Campos shut the door and shouted, "Johnson!" It brought a young officer with hair cut so short his pink scalp showed. He was large and solid and he came at a jog that jarred the floor. Campos jerked his head at the door. "Sit in there with him. Don't give him cigarettes. Don't give him water. Don't give him anything."

He moved off down the hall and into a tan room of tan file cabinets where a tan steel desk held two telephones, a shuffle of manila folders, coffee-stained Styrofoam cups, a choked glass ashtray. Back of the desk a tan metal swivel chair was upholstered in fake leather. He dropped into it and nodded at straight chairs that matched it, waited for April and Dave to sit, then asked her, "Have you seen him before?"

"Of course," she said. "At the hospital. He mopped, he pushed those big metal wagons they take away the patients' dirty dishes in, he brought bed linens, took patients in and out in wheelchairs, stretchers. He was on at night. Sometimes I'd find him there visiting with John. He'd always slide out as soon as he saw me." She gave a little shiver. "He reminded me of a snake. I couldn't see how

John could stand him. I supposed he was lonely. I couldn't be there all the time."

"Did he ever give Mr. Oats hypodermic injections?"

"Why, no. Only a registered nurse—" She stopped and stared. "Oh. It's about the morphine, isn't it? That he wasn't supposed to have."

"That's what it's about," Campos said.

Dave said, "You told me no one came to see him at your place. No one but Dr. De Kalb and Jay McPhail. You want to change that now?"

"You said friends. I didn't think of him. I guess I wanted to forget him and I did. Yes, he came. John hadn't been out of the hospital two days when he showed up. In an old wreck of a Volkswagen. I was supposed to think it was kind and thoughtful of him. I couldn't. I know it's not fair, but he makes my flesh crawl. I told him John wasn't there, but John came out of the bedroom to see who I was talking to and invited him in. I brought them coffee. But I couldn't stay in the same room. I went back to the kitchen. And when I heard him going I followed him outside. I felt guilty, but it was my house and I didn't want him in it. And I did admit it to John afterward. I told the boy not to come back."

"He came back," Dave said. "Did you see him?"

She shook her head. "Once or twice I thought I heard that rattly motor. After dark, while John was having his swim. I went out on the deck to look, but I couldn't see. And since he didn't come to the door, I didn't worry about it again." Her mouth took a little sorry twist. "I should have worried, shouldn't I?"

"You didn't hear that car the night he died?" Campos asked. "No . . . you weren't home. I remember." He sighed, stood, forced the tired smile again. "Okay, Miss Stannard. Thank you. I think we know where we are, now. He'll tell us the rest. Not right away, but in a few hours. He'll need help then and he'll talk. I'll call you. I'll call you, Brandstetter."

10

THE PHONE RANG. It cost effort, but he opened his eyes. Grayness trying to be daylight edged the curtains. He groaned and shifted stiff joints on the white couch. It seemed only a minute ago he'd shed his clothes—fingers numb from too many hours clutching a steering wheel along too many fast lanes of too many freeways—parted the white shutter doors to the hall and, moving softly in slatted lamplight, dragged down a blanket from a high shelf of the linen closet. He'd wrapped himself in it, switched off the lamp and dropped here, dropped into sleep before there was time to arrange his bones. He sat up, ran a hand down his face, shivered. His watch lay on the orange Parsons table. He picked it up, held it close. 6:17. It had been 3:40 when he got here. He pushed to his feet and stumbled through shadows to the kitchen. He unhooked the receiver and dropped it. It swung on its tether of red rubber-coated cord, knocking its mouth against the wall. He fumbled for it, recovered it, croaked his name into it.

"It's no good," Jesus-Maria Campos said. "It looked very good, but it's no good. On the night Oats drowned, this kid was locked up. In Oxnard."

"In jail? What for?"

Doug pulled open the shutter doors from the dining space and stood holding them. He wore a yellow terry-cloth robe, rubber thongs. His hair was tousled. One of his hands was wrapped in white gauze. In the dimness he could have been Rod. His eyes were like Rod's had been— opaque, shiny, like stones fresh from a lapidary's tumbler. Their look now was reproachful.

Campos said, "Stolen car. He wasn't the driver. He'd only hitched a ride. But he got held just the same. Till the next morning. It was sundown when they got stopped. Oats wasn't drowned till after dark."

"Right. But he did take the stuff to Oats?"

"In fifty-dollar fixes," Campos said. "The kid had close to three thousand dollars in his room. Oats wasn't the only one. Thanks for putting me on to this."

"*For nada.*" Dave hung up, turned away, lit the kitchen. Off the burner deck he took the coffeemaker, separated the parts, emptied and rinsed them at the sink. The doors stuttered behind him. Had Doug come in or gone out? Did it matter? He ran water into the lower section of the pot, reached down a bright can from a cupboard and with a little yellow plastic scoop measured coffee into the top section. The doors stuttered again. He turned. Doug held out his old blue corduroy robe.

"You were here earlier," he said.

"You were busy." Dave fitted the top part into the bottom part. "Anyway, I had to go back."

"You weren't coming," Doug said. "For undisclosed reasons. You were going to phone me in the morning."

"I obviously should have phoned last night." Dave took the robe and shrugged into it. "It's what's called discretion—right?"

"Sometimes it's just called manners," Doug said. "What made you change your mind?"

"A girl alone on an empty beach at night." Dave set the coffeemaker on its burner and twisted the knob. With a soft pop, flame drew a blue asterisk under the pot. Dave stared at it. "The man she loved drowned a week ago. She doesn't like me. I keep bringing her news she doesn't want to hear. All the same, tonight she asked me to stay with her. For a drink, she said, but she meant more. It was dark. Any man would have done. I just happened to come by. And—" He patted the old robe's pocket, wanting a cigarette. Doug held out his pack. Blue. Gauloises. Dave took one. "And it reached me how it feels to be left alone. By the dead. Really alone." He watched Doug steadily while Doug lit the cigarette for him, lit his own. "You know?"

"You know damn well I know." Doug shook out the match, dropped it in a red ashtray on the counter. "Better than you. Twice over I know."

He was talking about Fox Olson. After Jean-Paul had been killed, Doug had quit his job with NATO and come back from France to Los Angeles. And by crazy luck he'd found again the man he'd loved when they were kids. After more than twenty years apart. But in those years too much had happened to Olson. He and Doug had managed a few good days. Then he lay in the dark on the splintery planks of a deserted amusement pier with lumps of metal in his chest that made his heart stop. And, trapped in trouble deep as trouble can get, Doug met Dave.

"Granted," Dave said. "Well, it turned me around. I told myself all that's wrong with us is misunderstanding. That's not good, but it's not the worst. The worst is not having anyone to have a misunderstanding with. It's not ecstasy. But it beats nothing. So—I came home. A mistake. Or was it? Don't tell me now. I have to use the bathroom. Unless, of course, it's occupied by your friend."

"Lorant?" Doug's laugh was brief and ironic. He shook his head. "Lorant's not here. He wasn't here when you came home the first time. He left shortly after dinner. Left in a hurry. Which explains the jacket. It seems he doesn't sleep with men. It upset him that I thought he would. I hope there's another place like European Motors in town. I don't think I can go back to European Motors. Not comfortably."

"Too bad," Dave said. "Excuse me a minute."

When he came out of the bathroom he looked to his left. The bedroom door stood open. Beyond, in shadow, a white bed loomed. It was too big for the room. Wickerwork, of all things—whorls, sprays, serpentines. A joke, but built to last—not true of most furniture at the time he'd bought it, December 1945. He'd come back from the snowy rubble of Germany to the gray rains of LA, out of the Army but still in uniform because he'd fined down and none of the clothes he'd left behind fitted anymore. He couldn't see living with his father again, or rather with his father's women, and because apartments were scarce, he'd used money put by when he was a kid for a college education he didn't want, to make a down payment on a house—this one, old even then, small, on a dowdy side street. And he'd needed something to sleep on. Nothing so ridiculous. But he'd have bought whatever the clerk showed him, that particular clerk, a small, dark, effeminate boy whose name had been Rod Fleming and with whom he'd slept in that absurd bed—barring times of illness, anger, absence— every night since. Till death did them part. That Lorant might have put his stranger's nakedness into that bed last night made Dave's fists tighten. He opened them. His mouth twitched disgust at himself. A bed, for Christ's sake, was a collection of sticks and springs and ticking. And Rod? Rod was even less than that now. Dave turned and went back to the bright kitchen, where Doug was alive—not smiling, but alive—and holding out coffee to him in a big pottery mug, terra-cotta color, one of a pair he and Rod had always used at breakfast. He took it with a nod, Doug asked him:

"Do you know what I wished when I bloodied myself yesterday?" A cigarette burned in the fingers of his damaged hand. As he smoked, the white bandage lifted and fell like a distress signal. "I wished you were with me. When the doctor sewed me up, I wanted you there. And when I came home, I wanted you. Not a voice on the telephone, seventy-five miles away, promising to call me in the morning. You. Here."

"I said I was sorry about your hand."

"But you hated me for not wanting to drive."

"You fixed Chicken Marengo for Lorant." Dave set down his mug and shook a cigarette from Doug's blue pack on the counter. "That takes both hands."

"I would have fixed it for you." Doug picked up the red iron skillet from the burner deck, held it under a hard, hot spray from the swing tap. "You didn't want it." With his good hand and a soft ball of copper mesh, he scoured the pan's black insides. "And when you hung up, I thought how very different it was. Jean-Paul would have come. Because I was hurt. Not badly—just hurt. So"—Doug twisted the knob marked HOT so the spray stopped, pulled paper towels off a roll, dried the pan—"it was him I missed. The dead, right? Who can't come back." He set the pan on the burner deck, took the one that had held wild rice to the sink, splashed it full of water, left it to soak. "And I was like your girl on the beach. I thought of the nearest man." He opened the refrigerator. His laugh at himself was wry. "My choice was no better than hers."

"But you are not," Dave said, "alone."

"No?" Doug brought out a flat, plastic-wrapped pack of bacon, a carton of eggs, a stick of butter. "That was how I felt. I don't know how it is with you." The big door swung shut with a smack of rubber insulation. "With me it's an ache in the lower right arm. Why there, I can't say. But when it comes, I know it's real." He laid bacon strips in the skillet. "You forget I'm a stranger here. I don't know anyone but you." Bending to watch the flame, he turned the heat on low. "The days get long."

"They wouldn't get so long"—Dave reached down a snowy little can of orange-juice concentrate from the freezer, watched it waltz with the electric can-opener—"if you'd forget France. Scrap the records, throw out the magazines with his picture, get rid of the Ferrari." He shook the icy orange cylinder into the jar of thick glass that waited on top of the blender. "Cars were his thing, Doug, not yours."

He filled the little can with water, poured it in, capped the jar. "One of the first things your mother told me about you was that you didn't know a camshaft from a carburetor." The blender had stops enough to confuse E. Power Biggs. Dave pushed the one he was sure of. The little motor whined. Inside the jar, chaos began, like the explosion of a miniature sun. "You still don't. That's why you need European Motors. Be honest. Let it go. Let him go."

He turned. No Doug. The doors wagged. From its hook in a row of hooks he got down a square skillet, set it beside the one where the bacon sizzled, cut butter into it, lit the burner. Doug brought in the smeared table clutter from last night, stacked it on the counter by the sink, stood next to Dave to turn the bacon with a steel fork. He said:

"I've wondered what you'd be like, upset. I'd have bet on this." His mug stood on the brick surround of the burner deck. He picked it up, drank from it.

Dave took the eggs from the carton. Cradling them cold in his hand, he asked, "On what?"

"On how you are. Rational, analytical and ruthless." His look held Dave's for a second. Then he set the mug down and turned the bacon again. Dave broke eggs into the pan, one to a corner. Doug said, "The phone in the bedroom clicks when you dial out here. It woke me when you came home the first time. I waited for the call to end, for you to come in. When it ended and you didn't come, when I heard the back door close, heard your car start, heard it drive off up the street, I came out. And saw the jacket." He stepped across the waxed bricks to switch off the blender. "I thought a lot of different things." He took glasses from a cupboard, filled them from the jar. He held one out to Dave, hurt in the shiny stone eyes. "Most of all, I thought how gentle you are. But you're not gentle, are you?"

"Ruthless." Dave set the glass down, rummaged a spatula from a drawer. "It's a habit of mind you get into when your job is to find the truth and not accept substitutes."

Doug said, "What is the truth?"

"In this case?" Dave carefully turned the eggs. "I am." He nodded at the other pan. "You want to drain the bacon?"

Doug flattened a thickness of paper towels on the counter and forked the strips on to it. He got down plates and held them out, frowning, while Dave slid the buttery eggs on to them. "I don't understand." He turned to lay bacon on the plates.

"It's very simple." Dave refilled the coffee mugs. "Jean-Paul is dead. I'm not dead."

"It's not simple, God damn it," Doug said.

"Let's eat," Dave said.

11

FLOYD KELLOGG—TWEEDS, sideburns, briar pipe—got up from a desk barricaded by stacks of new books in flashy jackets. New books in flashy jackets crowded the high shelving back of him. Bancroft's on Vine just off Hollywood Boulevard was a tall, bright cave of new books in flashy jackets. Kellogg was big. His grip crushed Dave's hand.

"Mr. Brandstetter. How are you? Haven't seen you in quite a while. How's Mr. Fleming?" They still asked. He wished they'd stop. "Dead, Mr. Kellogg. Last September. Cancer."

"Aw, that's too bad. He was a young man." For a second, primeval fear showed in Kellogg's eyes. Then primeval relief. *Somebody else, not me, not this time.* "Can't get over it. I had some books piled up in the back to show him when he came in." Headshake, tongue-cluck. "Shock. Real shock."

"I'm sorry about the books. Shall I take them?"

"Oh, no, no, no." Squeeze of the arm. "I'll just put them back in stock. Not your kind of thing. *Hollywood in the Forties. The Films of Joan Crawford.* His kind of thing."

"Right." Rod would have cheered. He'd have torn open the brown wrapping in the car before they left the parking lot. At home, he'd have grabbed corn chips and beer from the kitchen, kicked off his shoes, settled with food, drink, books in a corner of a couch, feet tucked under him like a girl. He'd have shouted with laughter. He'd have jumped up repeatedly to show Dave this photo of Ann Sheridan sultry in five-inch wedgies, that photo of Barbara Stanwyck in square-shouldered mink, a Luger smoking in her hand. And Dave? He'd have hunched down lower and grimmer in his chair, trying to focus on *The New Republic* or *Scientific American*. At first he'd have glanced up to grunt at the pictures. Then he'd have snarled. And Rod, feelings hurt, would have sat quiet. But not for long. Soon he'd have started chuckling. Then guffawing again. Then: *My God, this you have got to see.* When Dave would have slammed down his magazine. Or thrown it at Rod's head. Ah, Christ, forget it. What was Kellogg saying? Something about a price cut on the James Joyce letters. "Yes, send them out. But all I'm really here for today is information."

Kellogg's eyebrows rose. "You've bought every book in the reference section."

"Not that kind of information. About a girl who works for you. Part time. April Stannard." Kellogg nodded. "Nice girl, nice girl. Wish we could take her on full time. Knows her books. Just haven't had an opening. She wants to work at the El Molino branch. Only two people there. What did you want to know about her?"

Dave named a date. "Did she work that night?"

"You could ask her. She's—"

"I've asked her. Now I'm asking you."

Kellogg stiffened. "Well!" It sounded offended. He heard how it sounded and said it over again, amiably this time. "Well, all right." He rubbed his hands, sat down at the desk, pawed among bills, checks, receipts, for a pair of Ben Franklin glasses. He probed into a green tin file box. "Here we are." He held a four-by-six card out to Dave. In turning, his left elbow nudged a stack of books. It tottered and fell. He didn't notice. "The dates and times are all on there," he said.

Dave put on his horn rims. The listings were in different handwritings with different ballpoint pens. There was one for the date of John Oats's death. The hours were noon till nine at night. He handed back the card and noticed beyond the desk a slim figure. Familiar but blurred by the glasses. He took them off. April Stannard stood there, books in her arms, the books Kellogg had knocked off the desk. It was routine at Bancroft's—picking up after Kellogg. He dropped change, sales slips, packages. The nearest clerk retrieved them for him. April wore blue wool, cut boxy, like a Norfolk jacket, and only an inch or two longer. Her blonde hair gleamed. She'd brightened her mouth with lipstick. But grief was still in her eyes. She watched Kellogg tap the card back into the file. She looked across his stocky bulk at Dave.

"That's my card. Why?"

"People lie to me," Dave said. "Not all people, but some people. It helps to know which."

"You thought I could have—" She broke off, glancing at Kellogg, color coming into her face.

She set the books down hard, turned fast, walked away.

"Just a minute." Pushing the glasses into his pocket, Dave went after her, knocking against browsers at tables, shelves. She moved briskly but blindly into a trap, a doorless corner of the children's section under the mezzanine. Fluorescent tubes close overhead here, glaring off the flat, bright colors of the books. He caught her arm, turned her, she jerked away, tear tracks crooked down her face. Her words came out low, trembling, very angry.

"Why? Why would you think such a thing?"

"I don't think anything." He handed her his handkerchief. "I'm trying to find out what to think."

"And you don't care"—she blotted the tears, blew her nose—"who you hurt in the process."

"I won't hurt anyone the way John Oats was hurt."

"I didn't hurt him. Why would I? I loved him. I don't understand how your mind works. You say he was killed for his insurance money. I wouldn't have gotten that. I suppose it must have been me he was going to write in as his beneficiary. But he hadn't."

"In my job, money is almost always the motive for murder. But police statistics put money way down on the list. And I don't like long odds. You were closest to him. Lovers kill each other with depressing regularity, Miss Stannard. For all kinds of reasons."

"You are a terrible man," she said.

Kellogg lumbered up. "Something wrong?"

"Miss Stannard and I are friends. We're having a small misunderstanding. It won't take long."

Kellogg blinked, worked his jaw, grunted. He took a nervous step backward. A pale little boy squatted at a book rack. His floppy gray T-shirt was stenciled PROPERTY OF SAN QUENTIN PRISON. Kellogg bumped him, sidestepped. "Well, look, it's not busy. Why don't you go out and get a cup of coffee?"

"We'll do that," Dave said.

She walked sullen, wordless beside him, head bent as if she were reading the brass celebrity names set into red stars on the gray terrazzo sidewalk. She wasn't reading them. At a corner, a big, glistening white stall had its front open to the street. While he ordered coffees at a high counter from a white-aproned girl-boy with a purple bruise on his neck, she sat at a narrow shelf facing windows cheerful with morning sun, her mouth tight, her eyes half shut in outrage. When he set coffee in a disposable cup in front of her and took the stool next to hers, she said:

"We are not friends."

"Did Captain Campos phone you?"

"Yes. That creepy boy didn't kill John."

"But he did deliver morphine to him. Where did John get the money to pay for it? I checked his bank, his former bank. The account had been closed and empty for a long time. I had my office check your bank this morning. You're broke, Miss Stannard."

"I told you that. What good does it do to tell you anything?"

"That card on Kellogg's desk shows you've worked more often than I'd gathered from what you told me—but still not enough to meet the going price for illegal morphine. Where did the money come from?"

"I don't know. Peter wasn't earning anything." Her hand shook, lifting the cup. "Sometimes we could hardly buy food." She sipped at the coffee. "I just can't believe John would have hidden money for—that."

"You forget—he broke into a drugstore to try and steal 'that.' Drugs do unattractive things to people." He took a new cigarette pack from his pocket, stripped the cellophane, thumbnailed the silver-paper corner, tapped the pack on the heel of his hand, held it toward her. She shook her head. He lit a cigarette for himself, tried the coffee. It tasted like cardboard. "Yesterday you showed me the mail that had come to your house since he died. Among the envelopes was a telephone bill. I'd like to look at that."

"Really?" Puzzled frown. "I don't see—" She didn't finish. She shrugged and gave a little baffled laugh. "All right. Why not? It just happens I brought it with me. I get my pitiful wages today. I was going to the post office on my lunch hour, buy a money order and pay it." Her handbag was soft natural leather lashed with rawhide thongs. Out of it she dug a fold of flimsy blue-and-white paper and passed it to him.

He got out his glasses, slid them on, opened the bill. Only two toll calls were listed, with their dates and times. He put a finger on them and slid the bill toward her. "Did you call these numbers?"

She peered. "No. And Peter only called the Stage—that's local. And, of course, John wouldn't."

"Why wouldn't he?"

"He wasn't in touch with anyone. I've told you, we were alone down there. The three of us until Peter left. The two of us after that."

"And sometimes"—Dave stretched for an ashtray down the shelf among yellow and red plastic squeeze bottles of mustard and ketchup—"only one of you, when you were up here working. Do you recognize the numbers?"

She took a quick gulp of coffee, set the cup down, frowned at the bill. "Let me think. The Hollywood one?" Her neat little teeth worked on her lower lip. She gave a sharp child's sigh, shook her head. "No. I think I've called it. Back when I worked for Oats and Norwood. But I can't remember whose it is. This one, though"—her face cleared—"'has to be Dwight Ingalls's. He teaches at Los Collados College. American Literature. He was an old customer. One of those John thought of as friends—till he didn't show up after the accident."

"Maybe he did," Dave said.

12

Mesquite Trail climbed narrow and crooked between steep slopes overgrown with orange-pink lantana, blue plumbago, stands of lavender joe-pye. Old oaks cast speckled shadow on the worn blacktop. Warmed by noon winter sun, tall, rough-barked Japanese pines dropped pungency. Back from the road, up scaffolded flights of paintless wooden steps, or down steps cut into the earth, old redwood houses, deep-eaved, dark-windowed, low-porched, half hid themselves in green winter brush. Magenta bougainvillaea glowed on a shake roof. Scarlet geraniums blazed in a clump of sun beside a shed.

Here a pair of goats was tethered, there a burro. Rabbits, a hand-lettered sign said. Fresh Eggs. Inside a paddock knocked together out of secondhand lumber a pair of dun horses turned their heads and pricked up their ears as he passed. With a scissoring of blue wings a jay cut past the windshield. A ground squirrel hopped and halted across the road. Dave tapped the horn, frowned, looking for a name on a mailbox. And there it was, outside a gate in a redwood grape-stake fence, where a bright red pick-up truck waited with its tailgate down.

He swung his car around and parked behind the truck on the dusty road shoulder. He got out, shut the door, read the lettering on the truck. SICKROOM SUPPLIES. A striped mattress lay trussed in straps on the truck bed. The gate hung partway open. Nailed to it was an enameled tin sign. FOR SALE. A realtor's name, phone numbers. DO NOT DISTURB OCCUPANT. He pushed the gate. Two men in white coveralls carried up toward him sections of a brown metal bed. Below, on a square porch where ferns died in hanging baskets, the chrome tubing of a wheelchair glinted. Next to it a pair of chipped green oxygen tanks stood strapped to a red dolly. Dave stepped off the cracked cement steps on to a thick mat of dark ground ivy so the men could pass. Then he went on down, the drooping branches of old pepper trees brushing his shoulders, dried berries crunching under his shoes.

Dwight Ingalls blinked at him through a dusty, bulging screen door. He was a bald, spare man in an old turtleneck pullover, old corduroy pants, linty corduroy slippers. In one of his hands was a sheaf of typed papers, in the other a half-empty glass of milk. A smear of peanut butter was at a corner of his mouth. He chewed, swallowed, frowned.

"Mr. Brandstetter? It's not one o'clock."

"I'm sorry," Dave said. "Getting here didn't take as long as I thought it would." That was a lie. Los Collados, tucked in folds of the Sierra Madre foothills east of Pasadena, was twenty minutes from the freeway. He'd known that, starting out. But to reach a place early meant you learned things you weren't supposed to learn. Mostly they were useless things. Now and then they helped. He made the offer he always made but rarely got taken up on. "I'll go away and come back later if you like."

"No need. Come in. I'm just finishing my lunch." He knocked back the rest of the milk and with the hand that held the empty glass pushed open the screen. "Can I offer you anything? Anything simple, that is. I'm down to basics. Crackers, sardines. Alone, you tend to let the larder go to hell."

"I know," Dave said. "Thanks—I've eaten."

The screen door lapsed shut behind him. There was no hall. They were in a broad, low-ceilinged living room, redwood-paneled chest high, white-plastered above. Built-in bookcases. Window seats. Arched brick fireplace. Chairs, couch, coffee table were Mission style, flat-armed golden oak, fifty, sixty years old. Comfortable, the cushions covered in good-looking plain fabrics. Vast would have had to be the word for the carpet. Oriental, rich plums and russets, scuffed in places but still darkly splendid. The colors repeated themselves in stained-glass panels above the wide windows. Art nouveau flowers and leaves.

"Sit down. I'll be with you in a minute."

Ingalls went away into the rear of the house. Old plumbing shuddered. Tapwater splashed. Dave put on his glasses and crouched to look at the books on the shelves. Wright Morris. Nathanael West. H. L. Davis. And Thomas Wolfe, first editions again, as at April Stannard's. There was a hefty volume of Wolfe's letters too, the wide backstrip in soft black cloth. And next to it, in hard-finish beige buckram, *Thomas Wolfe's Western Journal: The Lost Pages.* A slim book. He took it down, opened it. *Edited with an introduction by Dwight Ingalls, Los Collados College Press. 1958.*

There was no noise from the soft-soled slippers on the thick rug, but a creaking board made Dave aware of Ingalls passing through the room. He set the book back. The screen door made a wooden sound. Dave stood with a snap of knee joints. Outside, Ingalls said something. One of the truckers answered him. Dave pushed the glasses back into his pocket. There was the hollow bump of the wheelchair down the porch steps. Dave dropped on to the couch. The screen door closed. Ingalls came back.

"And that's that," he said bleakly. "That's that."

He'd left the milk glass, the peanut-butter smear and the handful of papers somewhere. He sat in a chair by a lamp that was a pear-shaped Arab water jar of hammered copper, shaded by a drum of rough brown burlap. The table the lamp stood on was crowded with paperback books, pamphlets, literary quarterlies. Among them Ingalls found a crumpled Tareyton pack. He dug into it with a thin finger. Empty. He twisted it, dropped it into a hammered-copper ashtray already glutted with butts. Dave held out his own pack.

"Thank you. What's this about John Oats?"

"He's dead." Dave scratched a match.

Ingalls sat forward to get the light. He nodded. "They told me at the bookstore. Drowned. A shame."

"He was a strong swimmer. My company isn't satisfied it was an accident. Oats and Norwood is a hundred miles from here. You still go there?"

Ingalls turned down the corners of his mouth. "I telephone occasionally. There's not much point in going anymore. The shop slipped badly after John left."

"It didn't look prosperous to me," Dave said. "Dusty. Gaps in the shelves. Why?"

"John was the bookman," Ingalls said. "Norwood really only went into the business out of friendship." Faint smile. "He was selling insurance before." Thoughtful frown. "Oh, he might have managed, I suppose, but buying John out hurt his cash reserves."

"Do you know the figure?"

Footsteps thudded on the porch. There was a shrill squeak of little wheels, a jarring of the hollow steps again. Ingalls turned his head toward the sound. Squeak and jolt, squeak and jolt, the dolly with the oxygen tanks went up toward the street. It took a full minute, a long time. Then there was a clatter and bang of metal, the tinny slam of the tailgate on the red truck, its cab doors closing, the splutter and roar of its engine. Ingalls kept listening till there was nothing more to hear. Then he remembered Dave.

"I'm sorry. What did you say?"

"Do you know how much Norwood paid Oats?"

"I only know that the last time I was in the shop"—he squinted at the ceiling—"a month, six weeks ago, Eve Oats was, as my students would put it, chewing Norwood out about it. They were in the back room, hadn't heard me open the front door. She called Norwood a sentimental fool for giving her husband, her ex-husband, too much."

"It went for medical bills," Dave said. "That and a lot more."

"Norwood told her that. She said the county hospital was where he belonged. A charity case. Since he owned no part of the business, had no income, he qualified. Money was being wasted, thrown away."

"Delightful woman," Dave said.

"She's always been the hardheaded member of the firm. Money is what she understands. A shop like that has to be able to buy when the opportunity arises. Which can happen at any time. Oats and Norwood had a reputation. Fine books, scarce books. Ah, I don't know . . ." Ingalls sighed, mouth a twist of regret. "Probably even with capital Norwood couldn't have kept things up. John did all the buying."

"What about Eve?"

Ingalls shook his head. "She'd know the price to pay. But not what to buy, when, where. You see, it's a talent, an instinct. Either you have it or you don't. John had it. And because neither Eve nor Norwood has, I don't think the shop can last. They used to put out exciting catalogs."

Squinting in the smoke from the cigarette fastened in a corner of his mouth, he shuffled printed matter, pulled out a saddle-stitched white booklet and passed it to Dave.

OATS & NORWOOD
*Ernest Haycox: West-Northwest Original serial publications/
first editions/autograph letters/holograph manuscripts/
typescripts and galleys with author's changes*

"That's the kind of coup John was famous for," Ingalls said. "He did it repeatedly. Not every catalog had a collection like that. But the individual items were always first-rate. There were catalogs four times a year. Since he left"—Ingalls took the booklet Dave handed back to him and laid it down—"there hasn't been one."

"They're trying to get something together," Dave said. "I saw a box of file cards by the typewriter in the back room. Books stacked up with slips of paper in them on the desk. Along with bottles."

"It will have to be a strong list." Ingalls rubbed out his cigarette in the copper bowl. "They've lost ground. People are forgetting."

"Not you," Dave said. "You went there at least once since Oats left. It was January third, wasn't it? The day he telephoned you?"

Ingalls's bald head gave a slight turn to the side. He watched Dave narrowly a minute from the corners of his eyes. He moistened his lips. "Why—uh—" He worked at a little uneasy smile. "Yes, I suppose it was. Yes, it was." He nodded a quarter-inch.

"And before you went to the shop, you saw him. At April Stannard's place in Arena Blanca, right?"

"I didn't know whose house it was. He was alone there. Yes. At Arena Blanca. April Stannard, you say? She worked at the shop for a while. Pretty girl."

"She says you never came to see him and it hurt his feelings. He'd thought of you as his friend."

"I'd thought of him the same way," Ingalls said. "But my wife was ill—had been ill for years. Until last spring my daughter lived here and helped me look after her. But when she married, I had most of it to do alone. It was a progressive circulatory ailment. Before it ended, it involved several amputations. Julia grew more and more dependent. I was less and less able to get away. I could hire women to help out, but not full-time. Professors aren't paid fortunes, you know, Mr. Brandstetter. And the operations, the hospitalizations were expensive. Ah, well"—he moved a hand impatiently—"you're not concerned with my personal woes." His eyes shifted for a gray second toward the front door, the porch. "And as you no doubt have guessed, they're ended now. I didn't call the rental people right away. Julia died ten days ago." He held up a quick hand, shut his eyes, shook his head. "No, no. Don't condole. It was inevitable. I was prepared, as prepared as one ever can be. In any case,"—he drew a breath and let it out—"I simply wasn't able to get away to visit John Oats in the hospital."

"But you managed it when he phoned. Why?"

Ingalls frowned, smoothed a brushy gray eyebrow with a finger, eyeing Dave. "I don't quite understand this interview. Your position or mine. Am I being accused of something? Ought I to call an attorney?"

"I don't know why you'd think that," Dave said. "John Oats became addicted to morphine in the hospital and failed to break the habit. He had no money, but he was buying the drug. Illegally. Expensively. I wondered if he tried to borrow money from you."

Ingalls didn't answer right away, but the wariness went out of him. He relaxed. "Yes." His smile was sorrowful, but not a failed attempt this time. "That was what he wanted."

"Did he get it?"

"He said he needed five hundred dollars. I couldn't manage that. I went to the College bursar and drew a hundred in advance salary. I gave him that."

"Did he tell you what it was for?"

"I didn't ask," Ingalls said.

Dave got to his feet, smiled. "So April was wrong. He had a friend, after all." He turned away. There was a muffled twang from a spring in Ingall's chair. He went with Dave to the door, swung it open for him. On the porch, Dave asked, "How long had you known him?"

The light from the yard glanced green off Ingall's naked scalp. He wrinkled his forehead. "Years. 1957? Yes, that's right. I'd published some papers on Thomas Wolfe in scholarly journals. I got a letter from Oats and Norwood, from John. He had a manuscript in Wolfe's handwriting. Was I interested?" His smile at Dave was admonitory. "That, you see, explains why a reader in Los Collados began patronizing a bookshop a hundred miles up the coast in El Molino. Of course, I went at once, very excited. When I saw the manuscript—notebooks, actually—I was even more excited. They were the missing eighteen thousand words of the journal Wolfe kept of his trip through the national parks in the West just before his death. Only about twelve thousand words had ever been found, but he'd told several people in letters that he had thirty to fifty thousand words written."

"You don't have to tell me the rest," Dave said. "I saw your book"—he jerked his head—"on the shelf in there. Handsome book. Must have earned you quite a reputation."

"It's the kind of thing a scholar prays will happen to him, but never believes can. You understand now that if I'd had five hundred dollars, I'd have given it to John. Gladly."

"I understand that," Dave said.

As he climbed the steep stairs to the street, a mockingbird in one of the shaggy pepper trees spilled song, spilled joy. His hand on the gate at the top, Dave glanced back down. Ingalls stood on the porch edge, peering up, but not at him. He was trying to locate the bird. He looked as if the sound gave him pain.

13

THE MEDALLION BUILDING on Wilshire was a sleek tower of glass and steel. On its tenth floor Dave used a slab door that had his name on it, trapped behind Plexiglas. The office he stepped into was wide. Its far wall was glass. A woven hanging covered another wall—rough, undyed wool yarns, earth colors, Norwegian. The chairs were slices of hide racked on frames of brushed steel. Two of them were goatskin, the fur on, white fur. Those were for visitors. Not that there were many visitors—he wasn't here that much. The chair back of the desk was saddle leather. The desk itself was oiled teak slabs in another brushed-steel framework.

He liked it to be clear. He even kept the phone in a drawer. Now a stack of papers lay on it. Frowning, he let the door whisper shut behind him, crossed deep tobacco-color carpet to the desk. He sat down, put on the reading glasses, shuffled the papers. No problems. Routine. They only needed his initials. He slid open a silent drawer, took out a pen sheathed in rosewood, slender but heavy, twisted out the ballpoint, signed. This set, the next, the next. Old men dying. Old women dying. A child dying. Seven deaths since he'd been here last, day before yesterday.

And in that time how many deaths had there been that
didn't need his initials, that with all the initials in the
world would pay no one in any terms but grief? He thought
of Biafra. He thought of Southeast Asia. He thought of
Ingalls moving gray and dutiful through that fine old
house, to and from a rented hospital bed that held his
maimed and fading wife, fetching this, taking that away—
days, nights, months, years. Who could number the errands
of mercy, the errands of despairing love? To what end? A
red truck rattling off with the empty remnants of a life.

He put the pen back, shut the shallow drawer, opened a
deep drawer, took out the telephone. From his wallet he
slipped a business card he'd picked up beside a rococo cash
register yesterday. He punched a button on the phone and
dialed the number on the card, a long number. As the ring
signal repeated itself in his ear, the door opened. His father
stood there, handsome, erect, white-haired. Dave threw
him a quick smile, lifted his chin. Carl Brandstetter came
in and moved to a wood-grained metal cabinet where bronze
chrysanthemums stood in a flame-colored jar. He took from
the cabinet a frosted pitcher, frosted glasses, ice cubes. He
shut the top door, opened a lower one for gin, vermouth,
olives. His white brows queried Dave. Dave nodded.

"Oats and Norwood," the phone said in his ear.

"David Brandstetter, Mrs. Oats," he said. "You were right:
John Oats was an addict. I'm in your debt for telling me.
He was getting morphine from a hospital orderly. What I
need to know now is where the cash came from to pay for
it. Prices run high."

"Well, it certainly didn't come from me. He left me
penniless. I always knew he would. Never get mixed up
with a charmer, Mr. Brandstetter. It anesthetizes the instinct
for self-preservation."

"Last night you thought he'd left you twenty thousand
dollars in life insurance."

"You're wrong," she said. "I knew he'd written me off and
written Peter in. I saw the papers from your company in his

room at the hospital. But I never told Charles—I couldn't force myself. That was what upset me last night—the effect the news would have on Charles, the effect it did have. He aged ten years in that hour. All the hope went out of him."

"I'm sorry," Dave said. "Let me understand this. He thought you'd get the money and invest it in the shop?"

"He knows the shop is all I have. Twenty-five years of my life are in this shop. There'd have been nothing else for me to do."

"Could he have been giving John Oats money?"

Her laugh was harsh and humorless. "Oh, yes—yes, indeed. If he'd had anything left after what he'd paid John for his share in the business. But it so happens that Charles was the same sort of victim I was, Peter was, even April Stannard was—though I'm not about to waste sympathy on her. Charles had given all there was to give right at the start."

"John Oats asked Dwight Ingalls for money."

"Who told you?" She asked it sharply.

"Ingalls. He's got problems of his own—or had at the time. But he gave what he could spare. I found out about him through a telephone bill. Another long-distance number was on that bill. I wonder if you can tell me whose it is." He gave it to her.

"Sam Wald." She sounded thoughtful. "A writer. Not of books. Films. Television."

"Thank you," Dave said. "Any word from Peter?"

"If word comes from Peter, it won't come to me."

"That's what they all say. All right, Mrs. Oats. Later." He hung up, got out of the chair, took one of the two icy little glasses off the cabinet as he passed, sipped from it as he went to the door, opened the door. "Miss Taney. Find me the address in Hollywood of Sam Wald. If it's not in the book, try the Screen Writers' Guild. Lay on all the credentials. If they still won't give you the address, tell them you've got a big dividend check for him. That will tug at their heartstrings. It always does. Do it now, please." He let the door close.

"I'd hoped you'd have lunch with me." His father sat easy in one of the goatskin chairs, martini on the floor at his handsomely shod feet. From a flat red-and-white box he took a brown cigarette. He slid the box away and used a gold butane lighter to start the smoke. "I'd like you to meet a very lovely young lady."

"I'll bet she is," Dave said. "They always are. But I have to see a man about a murder."

"To serve the ends of logic"—Carl Brandstetter picked up his drink—"it has to have been the son. I've never known you to get sidetracked."

"The tracks in this case meander. And there are a lot of them." Dave went back to the desk to put the phone away. "But my hunch is that if I follow them far enough they'll all end up at a place called Arena Blanca on a rainy night when a man went into the ocean and didn't come back anymore." He sat on a corner of the desk and lit a cigarette. "Nanette won't spot you at lunch with love's young dream?"

His father smiled. "Nanette is in residence in Reno." The smile became a wince. "All expenses paid."

"Why not be smart?" Dave said. "Save money. Don't marry this one." He took another swallow of his drink, trying to tot up exactly how many stepmothers there'd been in the forty-five years since he'd howled his first protest at life. They shifted in and out of focus—a face, a voice, a name, a scent of soap, the taste of a certain supper, a warm Coke at a dusty country filling station, laughter, a slap. His own mother was less than these, not even a snapshot, merely a name on a marriage license dated 1922, turning brown at the edges. He'd found it at age nine when he'd dropped a heavy carton of stuff from his father's desk during a move and it had blown with other papers across a lawn. He'd worn it inside his shirt for weeks and cried over it when he was alone, imagining he missed her. He'd been sulky and savage to his father and to the bewildered girl who was his lost mother's third replacement, a breasty, wide-eyed blonde child who lived in a pink kimono stitched with a pale-green dragon and in a haze of Turkish cigarette smoke. 1932. He'd grown tired of mourning someone he'd never known and put the paper away. He still had it somewhere. He didn't know why. What was his father saying now? That this girl was different.

"I'm aware I've made mistakes—nine of them, to be brutally exact. But even I can learn, given a few decades and sufficient humiliation."

"I hope you're right." Dave gave him a level smile. "You know how much I hope that."

His father rose. "You could come meet her. You'd see. She's very wonderful. You'd like her."

"That would make her different," Dave said.

His father set his glass on the cabinet. Some of the chrysanthemums straggled. He frowned and worked at straightening them. "You liked Lisa." He said it without emphasis. Dave stared at him.

Lisa's name hadn't come up between them in more than twenty years. Yes, he'd liked her. Too much, as it turned out. His father had resented the way young David ignored Barbara, Susan, Ruth. But when the boy had taken to Lisa—she was nineteen, Dave only two years younger—he'd resented that no less. For once he'd chosen a girl with more than looks—with brains and background. Her father had been a high-court judge in Germany. Till the Nazis shot him. Dave couldn't recall now what had happened to Lisa's mother. Her two brothers had tried to leave Germany and failed. Only she had escaped. There was mournfulness to her dark beauty. But her smile was radiant. So was her mind. And she'd been someone in his own house at last to whom he could talk about books and music, painting and theater—things that made a difference to him.

Thinking back on it now, maybe there'd been some justice to his father's jealousy. Maybe Dave had been half in love with her. He still remembered with good warmth their jaunts to the old museum in Exposition Park, to the sleepy white rooms of the Huntington Library, to organ recitals in the gray towering hollowness of a cold downtown church, to chamber-music concerts in a bare wooden hall in a west-side park where a beaky, balding Igor Stravinsky had sometimes twitched a baton—all of which Carl Brandstetter had made it plain bored him. So that the two youngsters had taken to going alone. And to political meetings that wouldn't have bored his father but would have angered him.

Then there'd been a little café not far from his school where he and Lisa had sometimes met for lunch—strong farmhouse coffee, the good smell of newly baked bread, rain on a steamy windowpane. Had they met that way often? Too often, he guessed. Yet, of course, he'd been no threat to his father. Even if Lisa had been capable of unfaithfulness, and she wasn't, he had no use for girls sexually. But his father didn't know that. If Dave had worked up the nerve to tell him, would the marriage to Lisa have lasted? Possibly. He hadn't found the nerve, though. Not till after the war, when Lisa was gone and forgotten with the rest.

He said now, "Is she like Lisa?"

His father's smile was thin. "As like Lisa as your Mr. Sawyer is like Rod."

"Externals." Dave shrugged and finished his drink. "Dangerously deceptive." He got off the desk corner.

His father paused with his glass lifted, frowning, pretending concern. "Something wrong there?"

"Some confusion about who's dead and who's alive. But if it can be straightened out, I'll straighten it."

"You could let it go," his father said.

"That's your style"—Dave peered into the martini pitcher—"not mine." He tilted the pitcher over his father's glass, over his own. It measured out exactly.

"He working yet?" Carl Brandstetter asked.

"The offers have all been for overseas posts. Too secret to discuss. But—at least until this morning—he didn't want to go overseas again."

His father started to ask something and stopped because Miss Taney opened the door. For sixty years Miss Taney had maintained inside a body like an assemblage of bleached sticks the spirit of a nerve-shattered girl of five. Her mouth never stopped trembling. Her eyes were wide with fright. She delivered all messages in a kind of whispered shriek. The more so now, in the awesome presence of Carl Brandstetter, managing director and chairman of the board.

"Excuse me. Mr. Sam Wald is no longer a member of the Screen Writers' Guild, but they gave me his address, just as you said they would." She held out a memo in a blue-veined hand that shook.

"Thank you," Dave said. "You can take those forms." She took them and fled.

14

THE STREET WAS a curved cement shelf, walled on one
side by white buildings, Mediterranean style, and on
the other by high curbs topped with railings of thick
iron pipe. The drop off the curbs was twenty feet straight
down to the red tile roofs of identical houses, another
curved shelf of street, and more red roofs below that,
among the sun-crested tops of reaching palms. Up here
there wasn't bare earth enough to yield much greenery.
Plantings ran to clumps of spiky Spanish bayonet and
stunted banana trees in the jogs of long white stairways.
Sam Wald's front door had sometime been enameled
black, but the coating had seamed and scaled off in
places. Dave tried a black bell push. It didn't seem to
work. There was a stingy black iron knocker. He rapped
that. At the end of the red tile landing a fat gray striped
cat woke from sleep in a patch of sun, stretched, sat,
began to wash. She reminded Dave of Tatiana, his and
Rod's old cat. A little window back of iron grillwork in
the door opened. A bloodshot eye looked out.

"David Brandstetter," he told the eye. "Death-claims
division, Medallion Life Insurance Company. It's about
John Oats, the bookseller. He's dead."

The voice that answered was raspy and defeated. Like a fan's who's cheered fourteen innings for the team that lost. "I thought death was supposed to be the end."

"Somebody wanted it to be," Dave said. "I'd like to know who. He was in touch with you. Maybe you can help me."

"I can't help myself." But a spring lock clicked, a chain rattled, the door opened. The man who opened it was short and pudgy. He wore a brindled gray track suit made for someone no taller but a lot thinner, maybe a Sam Wald of thirty years ago. The shirt pulled up. The pants couldn't meet it. A bulge of lardy belly showed. The suit needed washing. Stained deck shoes matched it. No socks. Crusty ankles. Four days of stubble blacked Wald's jowls. He hadn't combed what was left of his hair. His lips were dry and cracked. He moistened them with a gray tongue and squinted gummy eyes against the slant of afternoon sun. He croaked:

"All right. What the hell. Come in." He shrugged, flopped his hands, turned away. "Excuse how the place looks. Busy. No time. Can't afford a cleaning woman. Can't afford anything anymore. Can't pay the rent. That's who I thought you were. The landlord. Lived here three years. Son of a bitch won't trust me for a lousy month."

Dave saw why when he shut the door and stepped down out of the hall. The room had space and a beautiful shape. Parquetry floor. Rococo Louis Quinze chairs and sofas, good copies. No one cared anymore. No one had cared for quite a while. Dirty laundry strewed the Aubusson carpet, the petit-point of footstools. On delicate gilt-and-white tables stood open soup cans, bean cans, contents half eaten, sprouting mould. Cloisonné and Meissen were lost among crumpled potato-chip bags, soggy milk cartons, dried-out wedges of pizza, chewed, forgotten. On a white plaster mantel an ormolu clock had stopped, as if frightened by an ambush of empty vodka bottles. The smell was of decay.

"I had two Oscar nominations." Wald picked his way through the wreckage, heading for a short curve of steps with lacy iron rails. A dirty shirt hung off a finial. He picked it up, looked at it as if he didn't know what it was, dropped it. "But do you think I can sell a script today? Can't even get an agent."

Dave followed him up the stairs. In the room at the top a handsome period desk held a big electric typewriter. Its motor pulsed softly. Rolled around its platen was a half-typed page. A sheaf of typed pages lay next to the machine. There was also a fifth of supermarket vodka, a punctured can of Treesweet orange juice, a thumb-smudged tumbler holding what was probably a mixture of the two. There were paperback books. Wald picked up one of these, his mouth puckered in disgust.

"So look what I'm writing now." He held the book out. Dave took it, found his reading glasses. On the book's cover was a color photo of two girls in black lace bras and panties, kneeling on a couch, taking the pants off a sallow young man with a moustache. "Porn. Cheap porn. It's not even a living. But—I'm working my way up. They paid me eight-fifty for the first one. I'm on my fourth. That'll get me an even thousand. Just one trouble. They don't go any higher. They want product. To get it, they've got to keep you hungry. Nobody who wasn't starving would write this shit."

He took back the book, dropped it on the desk, dropped himself into the carved, gilded chair that faced the Olivetti. "I had years when I made a hundred thousand. A decade when I never made less than fifty." His hand went mechanically to the glass that held more than orange juice. While he sucked up half the mixture, he glowered at the words in the typewriter. He set the glass down, put his stubby fingers on the keys and machine-gunned a sentence. "Sickening," he said.

"You'd have to do one a week," Dave said. "Can you do one a week?"

"It's not a question of "can"," Wald said, and finished what was in the glass and picked up the bottle with one hand, the tin of orange juice with the other, and poured the glass full again.

Dave said, "It might be easier without the booze."

"Without the booze it would be impossible." Wald looked past Dave. "What do you want?"

A woman who was very thin stood in an archway up two steps. Her soiled lavender wrapper didn't cover her breasts well. They were full, rounded, like fine fruit on a dying tree. Her skin was corpse white, almost luminous. Her eyes were very large and took color from the dye of the wrapper. The only makeup she wore was liner around those eyes. She clutched under her arm a little stringy-haired, taffy-color dog.

"He wants to go out." Her voice was deep, the diction stagy. It made the speech sound like a quote from *Antigone*. One of the more tragic lines. Dave guessed he'd seen her. In a film. Or maybe more than one. She'd had more weight then, but the bones were what made her beautiful and the bones were even more in evidence now. Her hair was cropped. There would be wigs someplace down the hall behind her. If she wore one for a minute, he'd be able to put a name to her. A moderately famous name, he thought. "I can't take him," the ravaged voice said. "I'm not dressed."

"Get dressed," Wald said. "I'm busy."

"Take him out!" she screamed, and threw the little dog at him. It hit the floor skidding with a terrified scrabble of claws. It came against the wall with a yelp and cringed there, shivering, eyes sparks of fear behind a streaky straggle of hair. Dave looked back at the archway. The woman had gone. Back to her amphetamines, no doubt. Wald hadn't moved. He sat staring at the words in the typewriter again.

"Is there a leash?" Dave went to the little dog, knelt, reached out a slow hand.

Wald sounded dazed. "What?" The chair legs scraped

the floor. He got to his feet with a sour sigh. "Yeah, yeah. There's a leash. But you don't have to take him. Why the hell should you have to take him?"

"You're busy," Dave said. The dog shrank back into a corner, whimpering. He touched its head, small, delicate as a Sevres teacup. He gently scratched the silky ears. The dog quivered, but it didn't snap. It let him pick it up. "Where do I find the leash?"

"I live in a God-damn nightmare," Wald said. He went past Dave fast and down the stairs. Dave followed, carrying the dog. He watched Wald paw among unopened bills and letters, magazines still in their mailing wrappers, on a narrow gilt table next to the steps up into the hall. He found a length of braided leather. While the small body wriggled with anxiety, Dave clipped the leash to the collar. He set the dog down and pulled open the door. It tugged him out, claws scrabbling again, with eagerness this time. Dave could understand its wanting out. What he couldn't understand was that after it had relieved itself in the ivy geranium that margined the steps halfway down to the street, it turned and pulled hard on the leather to get back to the house. It pawed the cracked black door frantically to get in. When he let it in, bent and snapped off the leash, it streaked across the littered room and up the short stairs. It was as crazy as the other inhabitants.

Wald was rattling the Olivetti when Dave got back to him. He'd finished the page. He yanked it out of the machine and laid it on top of the others. He looked at Dave. "Thanks," he said. "I hate going out there looking like this. In daylight."

It reminded Dave of John Oats swimming at night. "What did Oats want when he telephoned you?"

Wald snorted a kind of laugh. "Money. Nobody calls me anymore except for money. Why do people always want what you haven't got?"

"Obviously he didn't know." Elegant bookcases lined one wall—scroll pediments, pierced fretwork doors, and beyond the fretwork solid shelf after shelf of rich leather bindings that glowed with costliness and care, decades of it. Dave put on the reading glasses and peered. Hallam's *History of England*, two stout deep-green volumes, hand-tooled, hand-gilded in flawless tracery. *Essays of Elia* in cinnamon-brown pebbled leather with a rose motif in gilt between the cords. Symonds's *Benvenuto Cellini* in glossy black with austere gilt rulings. Dave hunkered down for a look at the lower shelves that were meant to accommodate taller books.

"He knew," Wald said. "I'd bought a lot of books from him. Then I had to stop. Couple years ago."

"So you didn't go?" Dave asked.

"What for? It's all to hell and gone from here."

Dave stood up, took off the glasses, pushed them into their pocket, faced Wald. "You're lying," he said. "You went. Maybe not that time, but later. He telephoned you again. And that time you went."

Wald stared. "Who told you? Nobody was there."

Dave pointed. "That gap in the shelves tells me. Big enough for three folio volumes. *Cook's Voyages*, first voyage, first edition, in tree calf. You left them on the coffee table in John Oats's house at Arena Blanca. On the night somebody killed him."

"Killed!" Wald half stood up. But his legs weren't going to hold him and he knew it. He sank back. "Look," he said, and his voice was hoarse and shaky. "I went, yeah. He did call me again. And—well, hell, I felt sorry for him. No, I didn't have much. But at least I had my health. Poor bastard."

Dave shook his head. "No, I can't buy it, Wald. You're in financial trouble. But you haven't moved a single book off these shelves—except those three. If you sold this collection, you could live off the proceeds for a long time. But you don't sell. You'd rather write stuff you despise than part with the books."

"I'd sell her first." Wald jerked his scruffy head toward the archway. "Only nobody'd buy."

"So why did you take those books to John Oats? I don't know the quote from *Book Prices Current*, but isn't it high?"

"Not very. Forty, fifty pounds."

Dave narrowed his eyes. "A hundred-thirty dollars?"

"You're quick with figures," Wald said.

"He was asking more than that," Dave said. "A lot more. And he didn't need books. He had books. He needed cash. For morphine. That's a desperate kind of need, Wald. Why didn't you sell the books and take him the money? In fact, why did you bother with him at all?"

"I told you—I felt sorry for him."

"Sorrier than for yourself? You don't convince me."

"I don't have to convince you," Wald said. "Get out."

"Give me an innocent reason you were there the night somebody knocked John Oats over the head and dragged him into the surf to drown, and I'll get out. No—don't try. Let me tell you. John Oats had a remarkable memory. He never forgot anything he knew about anybody. Obviously, most of what he knew was harmless. But not all. He knew something that could harm you."

"Now?" Wald's laugh was bleak. "You're kidding."

"Oh, things could be worse. You could be in jail."

Wald turned in the chair to reach for his orange-juice mixture. He was clumsy about it. He almost knocked the glass over. Not quite. He got it shakily to his mouth. He drank too fast, choked, had a coughing fit. When it ended and he was wiping his face with his hand, Dave told him:

"I'm only guessing, but I'm sure you'll correct me if I'm wrong. You see, logically, knowing you were broke, you'd be the last person Oats would ask for help. But you weren't the last. For some reason, you were an early choice. The reason had to be, you couldn't get out of helping. I suppose he thought you'd sell some of your library. You weren't scared enough. You tried to fob him off with *Cook's Voyages*, not even a very expensive item. Nowhere near the five hundred dollars he needed. Plus which he was in no position to travel around peddling books. He got angry and threatened you with whatever he had on you, and you hit him. What you did after that was stupid. A man wouldn't go swimming in a rainstorm."

"Now, wait," Wald said. "Just wait, God damn it. I didn't do it. I didn't even know he was dead till you told me. Yes, he had something on me. I guess it adds up to grand theft. See, after I went broke I kept getting books. Not only from Oats and Norwood. From all the good shops. Charging them. Then, when I couldn't pay the bills, they cut off my credit. And you don't know what that is." Tears blurred his eyes, oozed down through the stubble. "I *love* books. Not books. These, for God's sake, are books!" He grabbed up the paperbacks and slammed them on the floor. "I mean fine books, beautiful books. I don't dream about women, Brandstetter. I dream about bindings. I couldn't quit. I went right on. Only I just didn't—stop off at the cash register."

"And one day John Oats caught you," Dave said.

Wald shut his eyes, tightened his mouth, nodded. Opened his eyes, sighed. "He was decent about it. Then one day he stopped here. Said he didn't get to Hollywood often, thought he'd look in. I guess, knowing I was hard up, he thought I might want to sell. But all he asked was to see the books. Naturally. It was our common interest, right? So—he saw *Cook's Voyages*. He'd heard it was stolen from Stagg's. I didn't know then he'd recognized it, didn't know till he told me on the telephone last week. I said I wouldn't go, but I knew I had to. I should have sold something. I couldn't. I got drunk and I got mad. I picked up the *Cook's*. He'd probably spotted other stolen titles too. There are others—much more valuable. But *Cook's Voyages* was all he mentioned. I figured to tell him to take it and do what he wanted with it. If necessary, I'd cry. Believe me, these days it wouldn't be acting.

"But—he wasn't there. I got lost trying to find the place. It's off the map and I was loaded. I didn't get there till long after dark. There were lights inside, but nobody came when I rang the bell. I couldn't stand out in the rain, not with those books. The door was unlocked. I went inside, hollered, looked through the place. He wasn't anywhere. Okay, that suited me fine. I left the books and cleared out. If I'd killed him, would I have left the books?"

Dave shrugged. "That would depend on how much killing a man upsets you."

"You're a hard-nosed son of a bitch, aren't you? Well, listen. I didn't kill him. But maybe I wasn't the only one he was putting the arm on. And maybe they had more to lose. Somebody was there just before me."

"Muddy footprints?" Dave asked.

"Better than that. While I was driving down that road through the hills to the cove, a car passed me coming up. At a curve. So my headlights caught the driver full in the face. Even in the rain I recognized him. Another old Oats and Norwood customer. I didn't know him personally, but we've spoken in the shop. Bald guy. Professor someplace. Authority on Thomas Wolfe."

15

WAITING FOR THE stoplight to turn green at Santa Monica and Western, he fell asleep. Only for a few seconds, but asleep. Those two and a half hours last night, this morning, hadn't been enough. An angry blast of horns back of him woke him with a jerk. He stalled the engine and made mistakes trying to start it over. He didn't manage it before the orange light showed. He got across, but the cars he'd held up didn't. They bawled resentment after him. He muttered contrition and drove the leftover quarter-mile home sitting extra straight.

The Ferrari wasn't in the garage. Doug wasn't in the house. Probably helping out at his mother's pet shop again. He walked heavy-footed through the sunset rooms, stripped, stepped into the shower. Wearily he cranked the handles and stood under a hard hot spray, arms out to prop him against the wall, head hanging between them, letting the heat soak in. It took away the muscle ache. In the steam he soaped his boniness, rinsed, then turned the spray cold and needling. It didn't wake him. It only chilled him. Shivering, dripping, he pushed the white shutter doors, thumbed the thermostat, then toweled himself, flapped into the blue robe and went to the kitchen for a drink. To warm him again, to start him over. Because he had to drive back to Los Collados, back to that beautiful, sad old house. To get an explanation from Dwight Ingalls, an explanation he knew wouldn't be any good. He'd liked Ingalls and felt sorry for him. He didn't want to go.

Fingers clamped on the cold neck of an Old Crow bottle, he stood glumly eyeing the red telephone against the wall by the swing doors. He could call Campos, unload the miserable job on him. But he knew he wasn't going to. Not first. Only last. He tilted whiskey into a glass, splashed in a little water, drank deep. He shuddered, shut his eyes. He bowed his head and leaned on the counter till he felt the good heat start in his empty belly.

He thought of John Oats alone in the morning kitchen of April Stannard's shaky pink house on the white beach, belt tight around his scarred upper arm, sliding a needle into a swollen vein, letting loose the belt from his teeth, leaning like this, eyes shut, feeling the relief flood in. At whose expense? *A nice man*, April Stannard's voice echoed in Dave's head, *a beautiful man, all the way through*. Sure. Dave nodded, opened his eyes, straightened. Grimly he swallowed another third of the drink. God forgive believers.

Because he, Dave, could not. That she rejected the ugly truths he told her didn't matter. It was what she'd made herself blind to in those months John Oats sheltered in her house, slept in her bed, ate her food, that Dave couldn't forgive. She had to have noticed something. It was such a small place. Peter must have noticed. It would explain his leaving. It would explain John Oats's refusal to tell the girl why. Which had hurt her, but not beyond overlooking. Like how much else? Dave shook his head in disgust, finished off the drink, went back to the bedroom to dress.

The chest sounded hollow when he opened it. He frowned, pulled out the next drawer, Doug's. Empty. He crossed the room, bruising his hip on the big bed, and jerked open the closet. His clothes—none of Doug's. The carton with the pictures of Jean-Paul was gone too. In the steamy bathroom he saw now that Doug's razor was missing, his cologne. The living room had turned shadowy. He lit a lamp, squatted, slid back a door of the record cabinet under the stereo components. His albums, Bach, Ligeti— but no Edith Piaf, no Jean Sablon.

He stood, pivoting. In the ell that led to the glass patio door, the white floor-to-ceiling bookshelves showed gaps. A sleek little white desk was in that ell too. He snapped on its lamp. Nothing. But under it, next to his gray-cased portable typewriter, was a midget wastebasket in bright swirls of red, orange, pink, like the couch cushions—and in its bottom lay torn scraps of paper with Doug's writing on them. Many scraps. He'd failed a lot before giving up. Dave didn't reach for them. He stood and pushed the basket back with his foot. He was going to hear what they said.

The Sawyer house was on the back of the lot behind the shop, under a pair of big, dark magnolia trees. It was frame, shingle-sided, low-roofed and needed paint. The porch was a square of cracked and sinking cement. It got used for storage. Heavy paper sacks of cat sand were piled under a sheet of green plastic tacked with clothespins. On the flat porch rail two cages turned rusty, one with warped perches, the other with a squirrel wheel. Three cracked aquariums collected dust. A black-and-white spotted dog sat, tongue hanging, in a corner. Plastic. An ad for canned food. Dave pushed the bell button.

Mrs. Sawyer favored flowered smocks when she worked in the shop. It was only a quarter past six, closing time, and she hadn't taken the smock off yet. Short, plump, she peered up at him through thick lenses. One thick lens. The other was carefully pasted over with a circle of white cloth. Years ago a not so tame sparrow hawk had cost her an eye. The other eye was bright enough for two. The way she tilted her head was quick, birdlike. Her voice chirruped.

"Uh-huh!" she said. "I told him you'd be here. He said not. He doesn't know you, does he?"

Dave cocked an eyebrow. "How's that?"

"You never give up. I found that out when you were looking for Fox Olson. Last fall. Seems to me Doug ought to have found it out about the same time." The black, shiny bird eye twinkled. Then she sobered. "You two had a fight, I guess?"

"Not that I know of," Dave said.

"Oh, you'd know it." She laughed. "Doug throws things when he gets mad."

"He didn't throw anything," Dave said. "I'd like to see him."

"Course." She stepped back, motioned him in, a nursery-rhyme hen. "You can stay for dinner too." Good cooking smells were in the air. "It's what I always used to fix him when he sulked. Ham and scalloped potatoes. His favorite. Cheers him up."

The furniture in the low-ceilinged living room was 1940s over-stuffed, with flowered slipcovers. The window curtains too were flower prints. So was the wallpaper above the white- enameled paneling. On a square mantel over a shallow fireplace that housed a gas heater, an old wood-cased shelf clock ticked comfortably to itself. Underfoot was an oval braided carpet, sturdy, sun-faded. Past a divider of low bookcases that prisoned china birds and animals behind leaded glass doors, the dining room had a round pedestal table with knobby paw feet and a fruit bowl. There was a plate rail. The plates on it were painted with game birds.

She said, "He's in his room."

Dave had been here for Christmas. He knew the floor plan. At the rear of the house he knuckled a door. No answer. He turned the knob, looked inside. Dusky. But Doug was there, lying face to the wall on a narrow iron cot that was covered with a patchwork quilt. In the dimness he looked very slight, almost a child. Dave's foot struck an open suitcase on the floor. Doug made a sleepy sound, turned over, groped with a bandaged hand to switch on a lamp.

It was an old gooseneck, wrapped with friction tape that had gone gray with age. It leaned over a knotty pine table scarred from use. A boy had put together model airplanes on that table, etching it with razor cuts. A school compass had scribed circles deep into it. Vaguely the shapes of stencils from 1930s homemade Christmas cards were outlined in splatters of red and green, bells, fir trees. Murky stains at one end memorialized a try at sculpting in wet clay.

Dave had heard the story. Doug had been fifteen that summer. He'd wanted to make a male nude. He'd wrapped it in wet cloths when he couldn't work on it. To keep the clay manageable. But also out of delicacy and fear that his parents would see it. Before they had, he'd scrapped it. After all, even if he'd been able to shape it right, a clay boy wasn't what he needed. He'd made a figure of a raccoon instead and given it to his mother for her birthday. For years she'd kept it on view in the shop. Doug didn't know anymore what had become of it. He said it had been pretty bad. Maybe. But he had talent. The watercolors that still hung on the walls showed that. He'd gone on to art school. The war had pointed him a different direction. He'd been in the Air Force.

He said now, "What did you come for? You've told me how it is and that's how it is."

"And you won't try to make it different?" Dave shut the door and leaned against it, hands in pockets. "I'm not worth the effort?"

"You said that." Doug sat up, swung his feet to the floor. "I didn't say it."

"You went to some pains to demonstrate it. You didn't leave a thing behind. Nothing to excuse your coming back to pick it up. So we could talk."

"You mean, so you could talk and I could listen." Doug pushed at his tousled shock of gray hair. Squinting in the light, he picked up his cigarette pack from the scatter of loose change, keys, crumpled bills, comb, matchbook under the lamp. "According to you, the fault's all on my side." He lit a cigarette. The ashtray he dropped the spent match into was makeshift. Doug hadn't smoked when he lived in this room twenty-five years ago. It was a seven-ounce catfood can. On the label a tom in hip boots winked and lifted a plumed cavalier hat. "You're a little short on self-awareness. People who are always exacting right behavior from other people tend to be that way." He blew smoke out of the circle of light, laid the cigarette in the catfood tin, bent for his loafers, slid them on to stockinged feet, small feet. "The mote in the other man's eye."

"Versus the beam in my own," Dave said. "Right. You want to try to extract it?"

Doug stood up. "No." He gave Dave a wan little smile and a quick headshake. "Too painful. And I never could believe that "I'm hurting you for your own good" crap. I can't believe it now. People who talk like that are lying. They may not realize it, but they like to hurt." He'd stacked cartons against the dresser. He lifted folded clothes out of one and knelt to lay them in the suitcase at Dave's feet. "I don't like to hurt. Not anybody. Certainly not you."

"You're going back overseas," Dave said.

Doug returned to the shadowy corner, shifted a carton, rummaged in another. There was a wavery oval mirror attached to the dresser. In it Dave saw him nod. "England. I'd have saved myself a lot of grief if I'd gone there in the first place. Straight from France. Never come back here. What the hell was there here?" Something was wrong with his voice. He tried to say it over. "What the hell was there here?"

"There was me." Dave stepped over the suitcase, pushed aside an empty carton with his foot, gripped Doug's shoulders and turned him. He was crying. "There still is me. I'm willing to fix whatever's wrong, but you'll have to tell me what it is. I know you don't want to. I know you want only to be kind. That's one of the better things about you, one of the reasons I don't want you to go to England." He gave the shoulders a gentle shake. "Come on, Doug. It's your turn. I won't hold it against you."

"Yeah, okay." The voice was shaky, but the nod was firm. He went back to the table, to the cigarette lifting its blue smoke up into the inverted white bowl of the lamp. He picked the cigarette up, drew deeply on it, turned to face Dave. "You're pissed off because I keep a few pictures of him, some music, some books. You keep a whole God-damn house that says Rod Fleming to you all day. He remodeled it, redecorated it, chose the furniture, rugs, color schemes, the faucets in the bathroom, even the frigging pots and pans. He chose that nelly bed. It's not me that's lived with you in that house since last November. It's not me that's slept with you. It's him. No, you don't keep pictures of him. But Madge told me. I look like him." He didn't want the cigarette. He twisted it out. "And you come at me about Jean-Paul. Jesus!"

"Don't start throwing things," Dave said. "Tell me what to do. List the house with Coldwell and Banker?"

"Yes. Get someplace for us. Not you and Rod's ghost. You and me." Doug shut his eyes. "Ah, Christ!" He dropped on to the bed edge, bent forward, face in hands. "I'm sorry. It's too much. It's a beautiful house. Forget it. You shouldn't have made me say it."

Dave sat beside him, put an arm over his shoulders. "Don't feel bad," he said. "You're right. I ought to have shed it all when he died. Madge told me. The sign goes up tomorrow, Doug. I'll drop keys off at R. Fleming. They'll take back the furnishings."

Doug sat straight, dragged a sleeve across his eyes. "Thanks. And now for the ungrateful part. I'm not going back there, Dave. I'm not sleeping with you in that God-damn bed. Never again."

"Right." Dave smiled and kissed the tear-salty mouth. "We'll go someplace else." He thought it would probably be Madge's. She had room and she'd like having them. But he didn't care where it was, so long as he could sleep. He'd never felt so tired in his life.

16

NOT MUCH MONEY had gone into the building of little Los Collados College. The architect, if there'd been one, had focused on utility. Red brick. Square corners. An even count of plain windows, plain doors. Like a child's drawing. But that had been years ago. And ivy had long since taken hold, masked the ugliness. The buildings faced each other across a long slope of good lawn sheltered by old oaks. At the far end, backgrounded by the worn tapestry of the Sierra Madres, a chapel aimed a mean steeple at the sky. At the crux of four brick walks a statue was green with bronze disease. Dave read the birdlimed plaque on its base. T. KNOX McLEOD, D.D. The founder. Dead 1913. He clutched a Bible and looked stern.

Was the frown deepening? Past his feet, along the walks, flocked long-haired boys in frontier moustaches and fringed leather coats, girls in tight dungarees and boots. Some of them smoked and the cigarettes looked handmade and not tobacco-filled. Transistor radios blared rock. Over it the loud, cheerful talk was studded with words Dave doubted the Reverend McLeod would have countenanced. Eight in the morning was early for beer, but in the green woven-wire trashbaskets he passed Dave saw yesterday's empty Olympia cans. He grinned and shook his head. 1913 was a long time ago.

All that was alive in the library was a hefty girl in a long peasant skirt and black tights practicing ballet kicks back of a golden-oak counter. She was judging the height of the kicks by the top of a wooden cabinet of index-card drawers. Her back was to him. The door made no noise opening, but she heard it close and got her foot down fast and turned. She had a creamy skin and it blushed rosily. But she didn't lose self-possession. She wiped her forehead with the back of a hand.

"If you have a weight problem," she panted, "you have to do something. I don't eat anything—I mean, almost literally, nothing. And I still get fat. Ugh! Look at you. I'll bet you eat all you want and you're thin. There's not an extra pound on you."

"It's a matter of metabolism," Dave said. "Don't wear yourself out. It'll only make you old before your time."

"I'll bet you're old," she said, "but you don't look it. How old are you?"

"A hundred and forty-five," Dave said. "Can you direct me to the College Press office?" She looked blank.

He explained. "A few years ago something called Los Collados College Press published a book by your Professor Ingalls. About Thomas Wolfe."

"Oh, I see what you mean. No, really, there's no office. I mean, the College doesn't publish all that much. What did you want?"

"My name is Eugene Gant," Dave said. "I teach at Altamont in North Carolina." He watched her. If she'd read *Look Homeward Angel*, she'd react. She hadn't read it. He went on, "I'm preparing a critical bibliography of books and articles on Wolfe. I'd like to look over the reviews Dr. Ingalls's book received. Usually publishers keep files of reviews."

"Oh, sure. Those are here. I mean, not out here." She waved tapering fat-girl fingers. "They're in the library office." She nodded at a far door. He started for it. "Wait. There's no one there yet."

"There's no one here yet, either," Dave said.

"No, there isn't, is there?" With a little shrug of her big, plump shoulders she came from behind the counter. She moved lightly, almost floating, the peasant skirt billowing around surprisingly trim ankles, her long hair drifting after her like smoke. She moved quickly and the breeze she stirred smelled of lilac. "Here you go." She opened the door and sailed through.

Dave followed. Desks, typewriters, mimeograph, Xerox machine. A green metal workbench where a big screw-down press held the glue of bright new bindings to stacks of old pages freshly trimmed. A harp of cotton string for resewing loose signatures. Tools with worn red handles for stamping catalog numbers on book spines. Above the bench, among trussed and tagged bundles of magazines, aged and ailing books waited for treatment on green metal shelves.

From a green metal four-drawer file the girl pulled a manila folder, handed it to him, smiled her one and only time and went away. He put on his glasses, sat on a creaky tin posture chair and for a half-hour attentively leafed through yellowed clippings—from newspapers, magazines, but mostly from academic and literary quarterlies. For twenty minutes of that half-hour he doubted his hunch. Then he didn't doubt it anymore.

Grimly he laid the folder on top of the file cabinet and went out into the library. The girl wasn't alone anymore with the sunlight through the windows. Students worked at tables, slammed catalog drawers, squinted at shelves. The girl was busy. Dave found for himself the thick volume of Wolfe's letters on a bottom shelf and crouched there, reading carefully the sad final pages. Then he pushed the book back, got stiffly to his feet, called thanks to the girl and went to find the bursar's office.

Through the shaggy pines that lined the road the sky overhead was as blue as it was going to get. But the sun hadn't climbed high yet, and down below the road, among its dense trees and shrubs, Dwight Ingalls's house was in cold shadow. Dave shivered and rapped the loose screen door. The redwood door inside it was shut now, like a sleeper's face. He turned from it. Above, on the road, a yellow school bus passed, its engine rattle drowned by shrill kindergarten voices. Downhill a dog barked. Farther off a rooster crowed. Dave heard the door open and turned back.

Framed by the screen, Ingalls blinked sleepily. He was barefoot. His hands fumbled with the tie of a brown bathrobe. Recognition didn't come right away. When it did, his hand went for the door as if to close it.

Dave said, "No, don't do that. You were seen leaving John Oats's place the night he died. You didn't mention you'd gone there that night. Why not?"

"It was—" Ingalls's voice came out hoarse. He cleared his throat. "It was the same situation. He called me for money. I took him money. It would only have been inviting complications to have brought it up."

"You didn't have to invite them," Dave said. "They're here. Yesterday you told me your wife died ten days ago. Ten days ago yesterday was when John Oats died. My impression was that you cared deeply for your wife. Aside from the time you had to spend teaching, you looked after her yourself. But that night, of all nights, you weren't with her. You were in Arena Blanca, a hundred miles from here, in the rain. What kind of hold did John Oats have over you?"

"Hold?" Ingalls's voice came out cracked and he was too white even for a man who's just wakened. His larynx jumped in his throat like a trapped animal. "I don't know what you're talking about."

"He was extorting money from former customers. Not borrowing it. Extorting it. You weren't in any position to lend him money. You said as much. You told me you had to get an advance on your wages to give him that first hundred in January. I drove away from here thinking it was kind of you. It wasn't kind. You were afraid. And you got more afraid. I've just talked to the bursar's office. Eleven days ago you withdrew another five hundred dollars. You gave as your excuse an emergency involving your wife. Right?"

Ingalls's hand went to the hook on the screen door, pried it up, let it drop rattling. He pushed the door at Dave, who took it. Ingalls turned away. In a dead voice he said, "Come in."

Dave went in. The handsome room was dim, chill with the dampness of old houses hedged too thickly by trees. There were shut-up smells of stale tobacco smoke and old books. Ingalls made no move to lighten the darkness. Dave wanted to see him. He bent and pulled the chain on the hammered-copper lamp. It drew wan circles on ceiling and floor. The light through the burlap shade gave Ingalls a parchmenty look. It went with the sickness in his tone.

"I need coffee," he said.

Dave nodded and went with him through the murky dining room into a kitchen where dishes had accumulated beside a sink where a faucet dripped. Ingalls clicked a wall switch, went to a range that dated from before the war, lifted a worn drip coffee pot that stood on a dead burner. Dave heard coffee slosh inside the aluminum. Ingalls lit the burner with a wood match. Shaking it out, he looked at Dave. Bleakly.

"You don't trust me out of your sight."

"The man who saw you leaving Arena Blanca said that when he got to the house out at the point, no one was home. He arrived just after you left. Oats had made an appointment with him. And Oats didn't have a car to go anywhere in. He ought to have been there. Especially since he was desperate for money."

Ingalls's smile was skeptical but thin. "You believe I killed him, dragged his body into the surf?"

"That was the night it happened. Did you have a reason to kill him?"

"Your profession," Ingalls said, "has given you an outlook I can't share. I've never been able to conceive of a "reason", as you put it, for one human being to kill another. My life for the past ten years has been devoted to keeping death away from one human being. To the best of my ability. Which wasn't enough."

"Maybe my witness is lying," Dave said. "Maybe he killed John Oats. Was Oats there to be killed when you left?"

Ingalls shook his head. Beyond the window over the sink a pair of butterflies played tag in a sudden streak of sunlight. Black wings with yellow borders. *Nymphalis antiopa*. The irony of their common name was almost too obvious here, now. Mourning Cloak. Ingalls turned from watching them to open a cupboard, take down cups and saucers.

"No," he said. "He wasn't there. Lights were on inside, the door was standing open, but when I rang the bell no one came. I went inside and called. No answer. I sat down to wait. I smoked a cigarette."

"Three," Dave said. "That adds up to a half-hour."

"It seemed longer," Ingalls said. "It was cold."

A built-in table between built-in benches under another window was spread with student papers, pens, pencils, open books. A red-striped cigarette pack lay there. Ingalls picked it up. He used another of the wooden matches to light a cigarette. Through the smoke he said. "When his body was found, was there five hundred dollars in his pockets?"

"He was wearing swimming trunks," Dave said. "The bathrobe he always wore down to the beach was on the sand. Soaked through, of course. There was nothing in the pockets."

"And did the police find five hundred dollars when they searched the house?"

"They didn't search the house," Dave said. "They didn't think it was murder. They don't think so now. Murder's inconvenient. It makes a lot of work. People do drown. They prefer to settle for that. That he was murdered was my idea. Should they search the house?"

Ingalls shook his head. "There'd be no point. I didn't leave the money. There was no one to leave it with. I still have it. If you'd like me to show you—"

"You'd still have it if you killed him," Dave said.

"I wouldn't take a man's life for five hundred dollars. Or five thousand. Or five hundred thousand."

"But you might to save your career," Dave said. "And I think you did. This morning in the college library I checked the reviews of your book. Most of them were excellent. But there was one in a Seattle paper that said Wolfe's journal was complete the way it was published originally in 1951. The reviewer had been a crony of the newspaperman who went with Wolfe on that trip. He'd never heard of the events described in your book. He doesn't think they happened. It was the only demurrer in that file, but it was there. Then I checked out Wolfe's letters. It's true he told people he had thirty to fifty thousand words in his notebooks on that trip. But the editor of the letters says he always overestimated. Is she right? Is the man in Seattle right?"

Ingalls looked at the window again. But the butterflies were gone. He shut his eyes and nodded. "Yes." His voice sounded hollow. "The notebooks were a forgery. John knew it. There was very little he didn't know about any contemporary American writer. It seems they were found in the effects of a man who died in Spokane. He'd been an admirer of Wolfe. He'd told his family Wolfe had given them to him after a typist had transcribed them. But in the package were three crumpled pages of what looked like a letter begun by Wolfe and thrown away. The handwriting on those was genuine. That in the notebooks was faked by someone else.

"A dealer up there had come into possession of them and shown them to John. The dealer didn't know that they were forgeries any more than the family did. John told him, but said he thought he could sell them. I was the first prospect he tried. But I'd examined hundreds of Wolfe manuscripts. At Harvard. At Chapel Hill. I knew immediately he hadn't written those notebooks. Just the same, it was a heaven-sent chance."

Dave frowned. "For professional advancement?"

"No. I was secure here. I had no desire to leave Los Collados. On the contrary. But there was Julia. That was the beginning of her illness. She needed specialists. It was terribly expensive. I'd already mortgaged the house, borrowed from relatives. Neither of us has rich relatives. So"—he drew a long, grim breath and let it out with a sag of his shoulders—"I authenticated the journals and advised the College to buy them. John set a very steep price, but I assured the department they were worth it. They spent an entire year's funds."

"And Oats kicked back to you?"

Ingalls nodded. "Fifty per cent." The smell of coffee had grown strong. He turned to the pot. It bubbled. He lifted it. The black stuff came out into the cups sizzling. "On the phone that first time—January third?—he didn't bring the matter up. But the last time he said he'd written out the details of the transaction, was prepared to have them notarized and sent by registered mail to the Chancellor. Or I could bring him money. I told him to do his damnedest and hung up. But in the end I lost my nerve. I drew the money and went." Ingalls smiled faintly as he handed Dave a cup. "It wasn't the best day of my life. But I didn't turn it into the worst, Mr. Brandstetter. I didn't kill anybody."

Dave set the cup down. "Telephone?" he said.

It was in a dim hall of bedroom doors. The room Dave could see into while he dialed was empty. Even the pictures were down. Darker squares on faded little-girl wallpaper showed where they'd hung. Ingalls's face, standing there watching him, had the same forsaken look. When Campos was on the line, Dave said:

"John Oats was blackmailing ex-customers to support his habit. Two of them were in Arena Blanca the night he died. One didn't have much left to lose. But if Oats had exposed the other it would have destroyed him. I'm with him now. In Los Collados. I don't know how you want to handle it. But I'll stay with him till you come or send somebody."

"Apologize to the man," Campos said. "Peter Oats walked in here yesterday afternoon around two. I tried to let you know, but you're never in your office, you're never home."

"Let me know what? What did he say?"

"He said he killed his father."

17

CAMPOS LEANED DELICATE elbows on a white Formica shelf and spoke through an opening in a tall glass partition to a teenage Mexican girl in a white orlon mini-uniform and kepi. She was backgrounded by stainless-steel kitchen equipment and bright plastic signs. BURRITOS. CHILI DOGS. TAMALES. COKE. SPRITE. ORANGE. Campos pushed bills through the opening in the glass. The girl slid a paper plate at him. She made change and rattled it into his hand. He pocketed it, turned and started for one of the outdoor tables where long-haired high-school kids and brown-uniformed motorcycle patrolmen already sat eating. He saw Dave and stopped. His skin was a dull clay color. There were dark circles under his eyes. The eyes didn't look friendly.

"I'm pissed off at you," he said. "The kid's mother told me you'd been looking for him. It was him you thought did it all the time. To catch the insurance money before his old man could take his name off the policy and write the Stannard girl in. That's a police matter, Brandstetter. You should have told me."

"A suspicion isn't evidence," Dave said. "I could have helped you look for him."

"Could you have found him?"

"I've got a lot of men trained for the job."

"Right. I apologize. Where was he?"

"He don't say. What difference does it make? He killed his old man for the insurance. That's all that means anything now."

Balancing food and drink, customers pushed past from the service windows. "You'd better get a table," Dave said. "I'll order and be right with you."

From the line he joined he could see Campos working fast with his little colored plastic knife, fork, spoon. His plate was nearly empty by the time Dave got to the window. So with his tacos and Spanish rice he took two Styrofoam cups of coffee. A black officer in a brown crash helmet had a booted foot up on the bench at Campos's left and leaned over him, telling him something funny. At his right a girl with long curtains of pale hair and pink granny glasses read a paperback book. Dave sat across from him, noon sun in his eyes. The patrolman laughed, slapped Campos's fragile shoulder, went away.

Campos lifted the coffee cup. "*Gracias.*"

Dave nodded, chewed, swallowed. "What did he want the money for? Just to keep it in the family?"

Campos shrugged. "He's at the DA's this morning. Maybe he'll tell him. He gave me twenty-five words or less." He blew at the coffee. "His father said he was signing the insurance over to the Stannard girl. The kid knocked him out, put his swim trunks on him, the robe, carried him down the stairs and out to the point, swam towing him out beyond the rocks, let him go."

"Neat," Dave said. "Can I talk to him?"

Campos worried his coffee. "It's not in the rulebooks. But"—he shrugged—"you clued us to clean up a mess at that hospital. The taxpayers owe you a favor. Of course, his lawyer might feel different."

"Court-appointed?"

"No." Campos dug a little clear plastic cylinder from a pocket. He thumbed off its cap, shook a green pill into his hand, popped it into his mouth, washed it down with coffee. "I don't know how they did police work before they invented these. Chemical replacement for sleep." He put the pillbox away. His laugh was brief and bleak. "My wife wonders when they're going to do the same for sex." His cigarettes came in a gold hardpack. He shook the box and held it out to Dave. "No, his mother got him a lawyer. Who else?"

"They weren't close." Dave took a cigarette. "I'd have said she didn't give a damn what happened to him." Campos clanked open a Zippo. The flame was transparent in the sun. Dave touched the cigarette to it. The taste was dark and rich. He read the box. "New brand?"

"You make them yourself," Campos said. "Machine costs a buck. Papers, filters, tobacco, another buck. My oldest kid started it and I smoked one and liked it."

"Making them must take time. Have you got time?"

Campos shook his head. "He makes them for me. I pay him forty cents a pack. That's a hundred-percent profit. He isn't doing anything, just laying around. He's too smart to be a cop, too dumb to be anything else." He wiped his moustache with a wadded paper napkin stained chili-color. He stood, stepping over the bench, made a fold of his paper plate with napkin, utensils, crushed coffee cup inside. Then he quit moving and stared past Dave.

Dave turned. Across the street, lawns, flowerbeds, old eucalyptus trees surrounded the building that housed the El Molino Police Department and city jail. White. Spanish Mission style. Central tower with pigeons. Red tile roofs. Up the wide, shallow front steps, between two beefy blond officers with big brown-handled .45s on their Prime USDA hips, walked a small, dark youth. The handcuffs that held his wrists together behind his back glinted in the sun.

"That's Oats," Campos said. "And I don't see the lawyer. Looks like now is your chance. If it's all right with the kid." He headed for a glossy white trash receptacle that was topped by a molded plastic hippo's head, mouth open. Dave pawed together the wreckage of his own meal and went after him.

Campos caught up with the officers and the boy outside a door at the end of a hall. The door was sheathed in steel, studded with bolts, had a little wired-glass window at eye level and a chipped enamel sign that read FIREARMS FORBIDDEN BEYOND THIS POINT. One of the officers tapped the window with something small and metallic. The other one took the handcuffs off Peter Oats. The boy's corduroy jacket matched the one April had worn on the cold night beach. Under it was a brown crew-neck pullover. His pants were tucked loosely into short boots.

When Campos spoke to him he turned and looked at Dave, who had stopped a few yards off. He was handsomer than in the black-and-white eight-by-tens tacked up at the old-mill Stage. Even the transparencies in Whittington's wastebasket missed the dark glow of his coloring. What none of the pictures missed was the gentleness. His look at Dave was the one the ex-carpenter must have given Judas after the kiss. But he nodded to Campos.

In the room with the blank tan walls where they'd interviewed the hospital orderly, he sat on one of the tan metal chairs, smoked one of Campos's strong cigarettes and watched Dave across the tan metal table. Steadily, gravely, out of brown eyes like a holy child's. The transcript of his confession lay in front of Dave. Typewritten, a carbon, three short, cold paragraphs. Signed in ballpoint by a hand that hadn't shaken. *Peter Charles Oats.*

"Charles?" Dave said.

"For my father's partner—Charles Norwood."

Dave took a breath. "You realize that under the circumstances my company will withhold payment on your father's policy. To you. But the situation isn't simple. It can get tangled and expensive. We'd like you to sign a waiver."

"Yes. All right." The boy nodded.

Campos squinted at Dave. "You mean you don't have to shell out at all?"

"When the policy was written, Mrs. Oats was the beneficiary. Peter was the contingent beneficiary. That is, if something happened to her, he would have collected. Then John Oats changed the policy, nine or ten months ago in the hospital. He made Peter the beneficiary—alone."

"So who collects now?"

"Unless Miss Stannard can prove John Oats meant to make the proposed change in her favor—the next of kin. Eve Oats, I suppose."

"It doesn't matter," the boy said.

Dave stared at him. "It mattered that night, mattered enough for you to kill your own father. You don't make sense. You arranged the murder to look like accident. The coroner's jury decided it was. Captain Campos here accepted their verdict. You were in the clear. You could have come back and collected what you killed him to get—twenty thousand dollars. But you didn't come back. And now you sit there and say it doesn't matter."

"In my place, would it matter to you?"

Dave shrugged. "You put yourself in that place."

"You were trying to." The boy leaned across the table for the ashtray in front of Campos—a little round amber glass ashtray. He stubbed out his cigarette in it, but he didn't watch what he was doing. He watched Dave. "My mother told me. You knew I killed him."

"That's not what kept you away. You never heard of me till yesterday. Or did you? Was someone in touch with you—someone I'd talked to?"

For two ticks of a watch the brown eyes widened. "No." The headshake was quick. Was it also scared?

"Where were you? Who were you with?"

"No one. I wasn't with anyone. I was alone."

"Just you and your guitar," Dave said. "That was a mistake, taking the guitar. It showed April you'd been there. That night."

The boy frowned, said, "But I—" and stopped saying it. He looked at Campos. "Can I have another cigarette, please?" Campos gave it to him, lit it for him. "Thank you," he said.

Dave said, "You had supper with your father. Not much. Provender was in chronic short supply at April's. It was scrambled eggs—right?"

"Yes. No. I don't remember."

"It was canned roast-beef hash. Neither of you cleaned up his plate."

The boy stood. "This was supposed to be about insurance," he said to Campos. "My lawyer told me I didn't have to answer questions."

"Your lawyer was right." Campos pushed back his chair. Its feet made a rubber stutter on the plastic tiles. He got up, twisted the doorknob, leaned into the hall. "Hayes?" he said. "Libisky?" And the blond boys brought in smells of leather and Lifebuoy soap and took Peter Oats away.

Dave handed Campos the paper. "This is no good."

Campos squinted again. "What do you mean?"

Dave stood up tired. "He wasn't even there."

"Where was he? Why did he confess?"

"That's for us to find out," Dave said.

"Not me," Campos said. "This is tight. The DA likes it. He'll like it even better when he hears about the guitar. And I got ten other things to do."

18

A SINGLE SPOTLIGHT bored a white shaft straight down through the tall blackness of the room. The floor it hit was painted black, so it didn't splash. Only when fat Whittington moved through it in a Russian peasant blouse. Except for red-embroidered hem, collar, cuffs, the blouse was white, and the light struck off it and reflected in the scallops of the varnished wooden seatbacks that boxed in the acting area.

Whittington stepped out of the light and darker figures flickered through like memories of the dead. Boys, girls, long hair, jeans, jerseys, play books in their hands. Seen. Not seen. Reciting lines, they sounded like lost children crying to each other in a cave. Dave went down the carpet-hushed steps, used a hand to shield his eyes, made out Whittington in a far corner, a swollen moon seen through smoke. He started around the dark margin of the open space.

Whittington called, "This is where you hear the willow whistle, Natasha. No, don't move—register. Stand very still. Then, as it goes on, lift your head. No, no, darling. Don't gawp at the ceiling. And don't swivel your head. Just lift it. Slowly. An inch, two inches, so you're staring over the audience. No, no. No expression. Blankly. That's it. All right. Now . . ."

His voice took a different direction.

"The whistle stops and Ivan and Marya start to laugh. Lightly. Pleased with each other. Ivan, you enter, holding both of Marya's hands, leading her, both of you still laughing. No, backward, Ivan, backward—don't you remember? So that Marya sees Natasha before you do. She's facing her. Go out and come in again." He looked at Dave. "Not now. I'm rehearsing."

"I can see what you're doing. I can't see what Peter Oats is doing."

"I told you the last time—I'd hoped it would be the last time—that I don't know where he is."

"That's not the problem anymore," Dave said.

"It never was my problem." Whittington folded his arms across the fat span of his chest and turned to watch the youngsters moving in the chiaroscuro. The Natasha girl began to cry.

Dave said, "He's locked up. He says he killed his father."

"What?" Whittington wheeled his big bulk around. His mouth was a slack gap of shadow in the blurred, pale bloat of his face. "What did you say?"

"You heard me," Dave said.

Whittington banged his hands together. It was a loud sound to come from a couple of pillows. The Marya girl was doing a mean little crab dance around the Natasha girl. She'd started to sing. She stopped with a little shriek. Laughter from the dark. Someone blew a slide whistle. It sounded surprised. Whittington told them, "I think the coffee must be ready."

He led Dave around the black partition and down the long room of beaverboard booths and costume racks. At its end, on a packing-crate table, the big shiny coffeemaker Dave had seen last time in the lobby showed a little red light and made stomach noises. Cellophane bags of cookies and midget doughnuts waited beside it with sugar, powdered milk substitute, a box of wooden stirring sticks. As if turned loose by Plato, the cave children came out of the dark blinking and swarmed happily at the packing case. Whittington led Dave outdoors where clean sunlight fell through the bushy leafage of giant eucalyptus. Then he halted and half turned back.

"Did you want coffee?" The offer was mechanical. Dave shook his head. Whittington frowned. "Killed his father? You said his father drowned."

Dave told him what was in the confession. "His father wasn't a big man. The boy could have done it—if he knew the fireman's carry."

"He knew it." Whittington sounded numb. A few feet off stood a ten-year-old Bentley convertible that needed a wash and a new top because the old one was gray rags. Whittington had lost his light-footedness. He trudged heavily across ground carpeted in brittle red leaves and leaned back against a dented fender. "I taught him myself. For a war play. He had to lift a black boy almost twice his weight."

Dave went to him. "And while there was rain that night, there was no wind to speak of. The sea wasn't rough. If he swam well—"

"Like a seal. But kill?" Whittington frowned, gave his big head a shake. A strand of pale red hair fell over an ear. "He couldn't. And his father? He adored his father. Charming man. I met him one night. Terribly disfigured. But after a minute you didn't notice. Later you remember him as handsome. Of course, Peter had to get his beauty from somewhere. Why would he kill him?"

"The answer that leaps to mind," Dave said, "is for twenty thousand dollars in life insurance. That night was his last chance at it. It was the only money his father had to leave. Somehow, through all his disasters, he'd kept up payments on that policy. And now he was going to cut Peter out. I don't know for whom. Probably April Stannard."

"Pretty girl," Whittington said. "I gather she and John Oats were much in love."

"Also she'd sold most of what she owned to pay his medical bills. And looked after him, housed him, fed him. Facts Peter knew. And she'd been good to Peter too."

"He liked her," Whittington nodded. "And he had a great sense of fairness. I can't see him wanting that money. Not really. Money didn't mean anything to him. Do you know what I often said to him? That in another time, another period of history, he'd have been a saint. It's only that they've gone out of style. There are no jobs for saints anymore."

"I'm not so sure," Dave said. "I talked to him this morning and he said the money didn't matter and I think he meant it. I don't think it ever mattered. Not to him." He looked hard at Whittington. "How much did he love you?"

Whittington's big face reddened. His voice went cold. "How are you using that word?"

"You define it," Dave said. "You were together constantly since last June. You kept his picture by your bed. You took a projector full of color slides of him. Before he had enough training you cast him in a big role in a moth-eaten costume drama nobody would stage anymore except to show off a pretty boy in tights. He was always here, hardly ever at home. His family, his friends thought he was obsessed with theater. Was it theater or was it you?"

Whittington straightened, swelled. "Now, you listen to me. I told you the other morning—"

"I'm more interested in what you didn't tell me. That the city has cut back your funds and that you're keeping the place going out of your own pocket. And that the pocket is nearly empty."

"And just how"—Whittington tried to sound steely, but he was pale—"is that supposed to involve Peter?"

"Twenty thousand dollars should cover operating expenses here for quite a time." Whittington stared. "You are out of your mind."

"I don't think so. Peter worshiped his father. Everyone says so. They were inseparable. Yet he left him. Flat. Very suddenly. No one knows why. But I think I can guess. John Oats had become a morphine addict. It changed him. He was blackmailing former friends. He even tried to steal from a store. Peter found out about it. It hit him hard. All that love wouldn't just go away. It would turn into something else.

"What if it turned into contempt? What if it seemed to him his father didn't matter anymore? And that you did? You loved him. A brilliant man, a famous man. Petted him, flattered him. And you were doing something, something fine he believed in, or thought he believed in. And for lack of money it was going to come to an end. His father was no good anymore, not to himself, not to anyone else. Why not have that money?"

"You," Whittington said, "are incredible."

"The setup here the other morning"—Dave jerked his head to indicate the narrow windows of the apartment visible through the treetops—"didn't demand much of the imagination. That boy in your bed wasn't Peter Oats, but he might have been. He was no nephew. He knew I knew that. And he knew how I knew it."

Whittington's brows rose. "Did he? Shrewd child. I marvel. All right. Yes, I wanted Peter in my bed. Wouldn't you? But hints and gallantries made no impression. So I staged *Lorenzaccio* for him. He was oblivious. I lost patience and spoke my mind. No. He hated to hurt me, I'd been kind, he liked me. But no. And—we didn't speak after that. The play closed and he didn't come back. Ever. If you don't believe me"—he nodded toward the mill door—"ask any of them. They talked of nothing else for a week."

"You said he was straight. Was he?"

Whittington pushed heavily away from the fender. "At the end, in my pain. I asked him. A mistake. I knew he made a fetish of honesty. He told me. No, he wasn't straight. As you can imagine"—Whittington brushed grit from his hands—"that made his refusal easier to take."

Arena Blanca still looked bleak. The cheery paint on the old houses, the glitter of the blue bay, the keen whiteness of the sand were lonely. The trim boats at the jetties waited like blind classroom kids, arms raised, with no teacher to turn them loose. Gulls, slicing the sunlight, were all that seemed alive. The weary lift door on the car stalls under the pink house still gaped. But the old station wagon was gone.

At the top of the shaky stairs he worked the buzzer and waited. No one came. He stepped off the worn rope doormat and lifted it. A shower of sand. He looked along the outer edges of the pink-painted door frame. For a small nail. There was no small nail. He stretched to run a hand along the top of the frame. The key had lain there for a long time. It was crusty. But it went into the lock all right. It turned the lock. He pushed the door and went inside, where the curtains this time were open to the blue stare of empty bay and sky.

She'd kept at her cleaning. The room looked the way it must have looked in her mother's day, the spooled maple glossy, the chintz slipcovers straight, even a bowl of flowers on the coffee table, California poppies, yolk yellow. A place for everything and everything in its place. Except *Cook's Voyages*. They still leaned like dark old tombstones at the foot of the wall of books. He opened the door in that wall.

Not far. It hit something and stopped. He edged through. What it had hit was another door hanging open. To a closet. He'd wanted to find that. He peered in. The jacket hung there, among others, the corduroy one, cuffs still turned back four inches as they'd been when she wore it the other night. It was exactly like the one Peter Oats was wearing, lined with the same gold check pattern. He crouched. On the closet floor, among other dusty gleams of leather, stood a pair of short boots. Same heavy straps and brass ring fastenings as Peter's. In his head he heard Eve Oats's voice: *They thought alike, moved alike, spoke alike, looked alike.* He shut the closet door.

The room was just big enough for a double bed, a chest of drawers, a desk and chair. And that was what was in it. All of it maple. The surfaces shone. A fresh white candlewick spread was smooth on the bed. On the chest with a chased silver comb, brush, looking-glass was a standing photo in a chased silver frame. A smiling man and woman at the rail of a ship, a thin blonde girl child between them, clutching a book and screwing up her face in the bright sun.

Except for a black portable typewriter case with frayed corners, the desktop was empty. But the drawers weren't. They weren't tidy, either. At least not the ones he opened, the top ones. What had lain on the desk had simply been pushed off into them—bills, empty envelopes, fliers, blue-chip stamps, pencils, ballpoint pens, limp rubber bands, bent paperclips, some dog-eared snapshots. And notes on scraps of paper.

He put on his glasses, sat down, sorted the scraps. Dusty to the touch. Lists—*milk, tomato soup, Spam, cigarettes.* Book titles. Some nineteenth-century dates. A lengthy addition problem in pounds, shillings, pence, the total converted to dollars, many dollars. The phone number of a roofing company. Dave glanced up. The ceiling was rain-stained. He smiled. He stopped smiling.

His fingers held a stiff yellow subscription blank torn raggedly along the perforated edge that had held it in a magazine. The blanks hadn't been filled in, but on the side with the printed return address was written Peter. And under the name was a phone number. He remembered the number because it had been hard to get. It was the number of Wade Cochran's ranch.

He thumbed through the snapshots. They were all of Peter. But only two were recent and one of those was blurred. He slid the clear one into a pocket along with the subscription card. He put away his glasses, pawed the stuff back into the drawers, shut the drawers. He set the chair back, put the key where he'd found it. He went away.

19

THE PINK STATION wagon stood drab in the sun on the blacktop oblong of the shopping center. He was moving fast when he noticed it. But the highway was empty. With a squeal of tires, he slewed the company car around and went back. He parked without worrying about the white lines and walked fast along the strip of cement that margined the shops, frowning through the sun-glaring plate-glass fronts.

She was at a checkstand in the Safeway. Jeans, Navy-surplus pullover, hair tucked up under a dark knitted cap. Boyish. He pushed inside, walked to the end of the counter where a wide black belt was bringing the items out of her shopping cart. Not many and not expensive. Just the same, she watched the cash-register tally anxiously while a stout, gray-haired black woman in a red smock worked the keys.

Dave cracked open a brown paper sack and began to drop the items into it. April looked at him. She didn't smile. The black woman made the register jingle and the drawer came open. She spoke to April and the girl took bills out of her wallet and laid them in the woman's palm that was the color of mushrooms. When the woman turned with April's change she saw Dave dropping the last item into the sack and clowned surprise, "Thank *you!*" Her laugh was chocolate with marshmallow. She turned, chuckling, to empty the next shopping cart.

"You were right," April said. "I hope it makes you very happy."

"Only moderately. There's something wrong." She reached for the sack. He picked it up. "You want to help me find out what it is?"

"Give me that, please," she said. "I don't want to help you and I don't want you to help me." He held on to the sack. "It could help Peter."

Her pain-dulled eyes doubted him, but she waited.

He said, "Ring the telephone company and find out what long distance calls you've been charged with since your last bill. There's a booth outside. One number I'm especially interested in." He shifted the sack, dug out the subscription card, showed it to her. She frowned into his face for a second longer, then looked at the card.

"That's John's writing. Where did you get that?" He told her, starting with the key above the door. "You have no scruples at all, have you? Prying—"

"If you'd pried a little, John Oats might still be alive. If you'll pry a little now, maybe you can keep Peter that way. Phone. I'll put these in your car."

"All right." She snatched the card. "I'll phone. For Peter. Not for you." She stamped off.

He set the groceries on the sandy floor behind a fold-down seat that leaked gray cotton at the seams. He backed out, straightened, let the door fall shut and stood watching her in the glass-and-aluminum booth, one of a pair in a notch between drugstore and Laundromat. The call didn't take long. She pulled open the folding doors and came toward him past tarnished metal racks that held newspapers behind coin-locked plastic windows. OATS YOUTH HELD IN FATHER'S DEATH. She gave back the card. Her voice had no life to it.

"He called the number. Or someone did. At five twelve P.M. The day he died. And now"—she yanked open the

station-wagon door—"will you please leave me alone?" The
seat leaned against the steering wheel like a defeated
drunk. She slammed it back, got into the car, pulled the
door shut hard. She was crying. "Forever. Please?"

Dave watched her poke blindly with a key for the ignition
lock in the gritty dash. "What did I do now?"

"What you started out to do!" She turned a twisted face
to him, scattering tears. "Prove to me that Peter killed
John. If that's where he was living and John called there,
it must have been to tell him about the insurance. And
Peter came and killed him. Isn't that what it means?"

"Maybe. But you don't believe it. And you don't have to.
Not yet. Not till I find out why the man whose telephone
number that is lied to me."

Las Gaviotas was at the end of a strong old pier south of
El Molino. Along the pier, white wooden bait shacks
shouldered white wooden souvenir shops and booths that
peddled fresh fish and fish to eat right there. There were
also taverns and a chandler's shed with coils of tarred rope
outside the door, a weathered dummy in a rubber suit, a
faded yellow life raft. Old men leaned at the pier's white
railings, fishing rods in their hands, buckets at their feet.
So did fat women in men's caps and bib overalls. So did
small boys.

Dave heard Mexican talk as he went by, Portuguese talk,
a rich infusion of Mississippi Delta black talk. Now and
then a car rumbled the planks underfoot, rolling slowly
out to the pier's end, beyond which big sailing craft rode
picturesquely at anchor, two-masters, three-masters that
hadn't sailed anywhere in years. The cars herded around
Las Gaviotas, a circular building with an uprush of neon
seagulls on its roof.

What they spoke at the tables inside was Main Street
Midwest. *Iowa* wrote itself on every sun-reddened forehead.
The skin around every pair of eyes was white from sunglasses.
Binoculars rested on corn-fed paunches in Hawaiian shirts.

Cameras in their cases kicked around on the tough green carpeting underfoot. Their owners ate crayfish they would call lobster when they got back to Cedar Rapids because that was what Las Gaviotas called it in red neon over the door.

Dave moved from the door toward the rear where a crisscross of beams was hung with heavy nets and Japanese fishing floats of colored glass. He wanted the kitchen swing doors the nets were meant to hide. When he was halfway down the room he saw a man with menus under his arm start toward him. Beautiful suit, crinkly red hair. His smile was all right, but he wouldn't answer questions. Not without sparring first. And maybe not at all. Dave nodded to tell the man he had legitimate business back there and lengthened his stride. The man had other things to do. He didn't follow.

In the pan clatter, the shouts, the steam and throat-grabbing food smells of the big sheet-metal kitchen Dave found a Mexican with a seamed brown face under his white paper chef's hat who was laughing with a pretty Chinese boy while they deveined shrimp at a zinc counter. Dave didn't use any preliminaries but a grin and the lift of a hand. He didn't like to cut the Chinese boy out, but he wanted to cut himself in, so he used Spanish.

"*Conoce usted a Wade Cochran, la estrella de television?*"

"*Si.*" The Mexican's grin widened. His nod was eager. "The Sky Pilot. I always watch it."

That came packaged in English. Dave went back to English. "Tell me—has he ever been in here?"

"He was in here every night a few weeks back. I never seen him. I work days. I got to get my sleep. But I heard about him. He come in real late. That figures. There is almost nobody here then except in the bar. Stars—they want privacy."

"But he came to eat," the Chinese boy said. "He doesn't drink. I mean in real life. He doesn't drink."

"Did you see him?" Dave asked.

"Once. I happened to stop with my girl after a film. I don't go around chasing celebrities."

"Was he alone?"

"No. Some dude was with him. I don't know his name. He went to EMSC. I used to see him on campus."

The Mexican said, "I heard he was always with him." Dave took out the snapshot. "Is this the dude?"

"Yeah." The Chinese boy stopped smiling. "I guess so. Are you a cop or something?"

"Or something," Dave said. "Thanks."

North of El Molino motels lined the highway, bowling alleys, drive-in movies, flash restaurants of stone, beams, slanted glass. He picked the motel farthest out, where a few live oaks still grew and you could see the hills bright with new green. When he got out of the car he heard a meadowlark. He stopped for fifteen seconds to listen, then pushed into an office so new it smelled of the glue that held the fake wood paneling to the walls. There were neat mini-jungles of plastic tropical plants hard-surfaced as the shiny floor. Plastic music murmured from ceiling speakers. Plastic air came down cold from ceiling vents.

The woman back of the counter had been the kind of plump little girl whose cheeks grandfathers loved to pinch. But that was in 1915. She was still plump, but the peach bloom of the cheeks was painted on now. The eyes were still round, blue, wistful, but the lashes were false. Her wig was a naughty toss of golden ringlets. The dimpled smile she gave him showed teeth little-girl perfect that had never belonged to any little girl.

"Isn't this a pretty day?" The voice was four years old, even to the lisp. "Don't you just love Southern California?"

"What there is left of it," Dave said. "I'm a representative of Mr. Wade Cochran. He stayed the night at a motel along here a few weeks ago. But he doesn't remember which one. What he does remember at this late date is that he left an attaché case behind. I wonder if this is the place."

"Why, yes." She was thrilled. She twittered. "Yes, it was.

It was very late, of course, and I wasn't on duty. Mr. Fitch, our night manager—he was here. And of course, he told me all about it. We all love Wade Cochran. Don't you?"

"He makes it easy," Dave said.

"Well, of course, he's so famous that Mr. Fitch knew him right away. He signed another name, but that's only natural. Celebrities like that have to do everything they can to protect their anonymity. So Mr. Fitch just let it go by. He understood."

"The attaché case?" Dave said.

The light went out of her face. "Well, now, that's a mystery. I didn't hear anything about that. And there's no attaché case in the left-luggage room. I'm sure of that. I know everything that's in there."

"I see," Dave said. "Well, maybe the young man that was with him that night has it."

"Yes. Maybe. Mr. Fitch was wondering about him. He didn't come in, but Mr. Fitch saw him go into the unit with Mr. Cochran. He said he was a very handsome boy. But he didn't know him. Is he an actor?"

"Oh, yes," Dave said. "Quite a little actor."

20

IN FRONT OF the white ranch house with its low shake roof, long porch, window boxes of red geraniums, the old oaks dropped speckled shadow on five cars. The evangelist's Lincoln limousine was gone. Instead there was a tomato-red Corvette, a bronze Nova and a boxy white panel truck lettered in crisp black with the name of an electronics manufacturer.

The broad-beamed estate wagon was still there. And so was the yellow Lotus.

Dave parked next to the truck, got out and shut the door quietly. The valley was a scoop of sunlit silence. Someplace far off a crow cawed three times and stopped. Then, nearer, a typewriter rattled. The motor of a small electric tool whined. Dave went to the Lotus and knelt on the flagging, which was clean except for a scatter of brittle brown oak leaves. He reached up under the left rear fender and scraped with a fingernail. When he brought his hand out, it was salted with white sand.

"Hold it right there."

The accent was Southwest. Dave saw cowboy boots, warped up at the toes, run over at the heels, matted underneath with dried manure and straw. A pair of short bow legs in worn Levi's. A faded blue workshirt dark with sweat under the arms. A leather-brown face, clean-shaven, broad-cheekboned. A weathered Stetson pushed back on hair that was Indian straight, Indian black. Narrow eyes that glittered like basalt. And a revolver in a work-gnarled hand.

"Stand up and state your business."

"Insurance claims investigator." Dave stood and brushed away the sand. "Medallion Life. If you'll let me reach for it, I'll show you my identification."

"I don't give a damn for your identification. I want to know what you want."

"I want to talk to Mr. Cochran."

"He ain't here."

"His car is here." Dave touched the yellow paint.

"He didn't take a car. He took a horse."

"When do you expect him?"

"I don't know, but you're not going to be here. Either you're going to climb back in that car of yours and high-tail it out of here just to oblige me, or the Sheriff can come and ride you away in his car. Then if you still want to pay Mr. Cochran a visit, you phone ahead next time and make an appointment. And when you come to keep it, go straight to the door. Don't sneak around fooling with his car. Come on." The gun barrel nudged the air. "Move it out."

"I think I'd better talk to Mrs. Cochran."

"Mrs. Cochran's a sick old blind lady. She ain't got strength to waste on strangers."

"I'm not a stranger. I was here a couple of days ago. You saw me. On the porch with the dog, the red setter. When you came riding in at the gate."

"Scratching a dog's ears and tampering with a car's two different things."

"All right." Dave pushed hands into pockets and leaned back against the Lotus. "Phone the Sheriff. I need him more than you do. And if you call him, it'll save me a dime."

The man squinted. "What do you need him for?"

"I'm investigating a murder," Dave said. "And now I'm up

against a gun. I don't have a gun. The Sheriff has. Or maybe you don't want him to find out a murder investigation is taking place on Wade Cochran's ranch. He might not be able to resist the chance to see himself on the six-o'clock news."

The man scowled and moved his tongue around his teeth inside his clamped mouth. He took a breath. "All right. Step up on the porch there." He twitched the gun barrel again. "And press the doorbell."

Katy wore a starchy shirtmaker dress again, but this one was blue. It changed the color of her eyes, but nothing else was different. Her frizzy red hair was still pulled back tight and knotted and a yellow pencil was still stuck into the knot. She looked at the gun, at Dave, at the brown man.

"What's the trouble, Hank?"

"Caught this man tampering with the Lotus."

"What?" It was the farm-wife voice of the old woman from someplace out of sight. "What?"

Katy glanced over her shoulder. "It's all right, Mother Cochran. I'll handle it." She studied Dave. "Medallion sells nothing but life insurance, Mr. Brandstetter. And you investigate deaths—isn't that what's on your business card? Deaths—not automobiles."

"I'm investigating a death," Dave said. "A drowning with violence. It happened at a place called Arena Blanca. That's Spanish for white sand. It rained that night. White sand is caked under the fenders of Mr. Cochran's car. Does he let other people drive it?"

"Drive it!" Hank snorted. "Hell, he don't even let 'em touch it. Me included. And I run this ranch for him. He even washes it himself."

"Not thoroughly," Dave said. "Don't fire. I'm going to take a photograph out of my pocket."

"Hank?" The old woman's voice came sharply. "Have you got that six-shooter out again?"

"This is serious, ma'am," Hank called. He growled at Dave, "All right, take it out, but slow."

"I'd like you both to look at it," Dave said. "Did you ever see this boy? Was he ever here at the ranch?"

Katy reached for the snapshot, frowned at it, shook her head, passed it to Hank. He held the gun level with Dave's gut and took three steps backward on the green porch boards. His hard eyes dropped for a wary second to the little curled square of glossed paper. Then they were on Dave again. The shabby boots came back. He held the snapshot out. "Nope. Never."

Chromed wire spokes glittered at the edge of the door Katy held half open. The old woman said, "What's all this about?" Finger twisted by arthritis gripped the door and swung it wider. Her bones looked strong, but the flesh on them was wasted. She was smaller than Dave had thought. At her withered throat was a fine old silver brooch. A bright afghan covered her legs. Open on it lay a big book in Braille, the stiff pages sand-color. She turned up to them a face honed by prairie wind and sun. The question came sharp from crinkled lips held to shape by expensive dentures. "You say somebody used my son's car?"

"Hank here doesn't think so," Dave said.

"I heard what he said. Nothing wrong with my ears. This Arena Blanca the only place you know of that's got white sand?"

"It's the only place I know of where John Oats was killed. And the day he was killed was the only day it's rained in the past month. And on that day he telephoned here." Dave looked at Katy and named the date and time. "It's on his telephone bill. Do you keep a record of incoming calls?"

"Yes, but I really think Mr. Cochran ought—"

"Go look it up, Katy," the old woman said.

And Katy went, brisk and prim, across the handsome pegged floors and out through the double doors that had fern patterns etched in their long, milky panes. She left the doors open. Beyond them the sun sparkled on the blue water of the swimming pool. At the pool's near end a pair of Japanese boys in white lab smocks were taking the entrails out of the video tape equipment. At the side of the pool a hawk-faced young man in a shirt with rosebud stripes rattled a Selectric on the redwood table while a man with a gray chin beard leaned over the back of his chair, craning to read the words he typed.

The old woman turned the flat black mirror surfaces of her glasses toward Dave. "I don't know what your game is, but I think you're bluffing. I never heard of any John Oats and my son tells me everything. Always has."

"Then maybe it wasn't your son who got the call," Dave said. "Maybe it was Peter Oats. He did tell you about Peter Oats, didn't he? Almost every night for two weeks he was in El Molino to watch Peter Oats in a play. And almost every night after the play they went to dinner together. And the night after the last performance of the play they spent together in a motel. Then Peter left home. And a note from his father's desk has the boy's name on it. With the phone number of this ranch."

"Hank," the old woman said. "Go get Wade."

"But he's at the lodge," Hank protested. "You know he don't let anybody bother him there. If I show up there, he'll have my hide."

"He'll come here to me," she snapped. "He's got some tall explaining to do. Now, get a move on."

"Ma'am, I don't want to leave you unprotected."

"Don't talk like a bigger fool than you are. There's four men out there by the pool. And there's three more out and around the place working. I can still yell if I need to."

"Yes, ma'am." Hank glowered at Dave. "All right." He wheeled and bow-legged off on his round-heeled boots, the gun hanging from his hand like a thing to be thrown away. He disappeared around the corner of the house.

"Why send him?" Dave asked. "Why not phone?"

"There's no phone at the lodge. No electricity. Running water from a well with a fuel- powered pump. Cost a fortune. But that's all. It's Wade's private place. A man public as he is—you don't know what that's like. And he's a spiritual man. He's got to be able to get away by himself. Just him and his Lord. Built this ranch for that to start with, get clean away from Hollywood. But it didn't work, not for long. Pretty soon he was busier here than he'd been in town. His writers are out there now. He was to be back down here for lunch and a story conference with them at noon. And to test out that machine that's being fixed before the mechanics can get away." She frowned. "Queer. Not like Wade not to—" The fern-pattern doors rattled, closing. The old woman turned her head. "Katy— that you?"

"Yes." She came back between the tufted horsehair chairs, the marble-top tables, the ruby-glass coal-oil lamps. She said stiffly to Dave, "John Oats did call. On the day you said, at the time."

"Who—?" His throat felt dry. He swallowed. "Who did he ask for?"

"What do you mean?" A line appeared between the pale-red eyebrows. "Mr. Cochran, of course."

"Not of course," Dave said. "He could have asked for his son. Peter Oats. The boy in that snapshot I showed you. Is it written down that he asked for Mr. Cochran?"

"It is. But even if it wasn't, why would he ask for someone who wasn't here? I told you—"

"I remember what you told me. And I remember that Mr. Cochran doesn't allow you to lie. Are there any more notations about the call?"

"There aren't, but when I looked at the memo, I remembered it. This is an unlisted number and hard to get"—she gave him a tight little smile—"as you know. His name meant nothing to me. I told him so. He said if Mr. Cochran heard it, he'd talk to him. I put the phone on hold and went and found Mr. Cochran. He took the call. In his bedroom. Then he drove off."

"Right." Dave felt sick. He bent and touched the old woman's knotted hand. "Thank you, Mrs. Cochran. I'll be on my way now."

"No." She caught his wrist. Her grip was painfully strong. "You wanted to see Wade."

"Hank just rode out that gate on a horse," Dave said. "He told me your son left here on a horse."

"There's no way into the lodge by car."

"And how far is it? How long will it take?"

"An hour up, an hour back. But you wait. You have to hear his explanation."

"It wouldn't explain anything," Dave said.

"Wade Cochran never did a wrong thing in his life!" she cried. "You don't know him. I do."

He said, "To love somebody isn't necessarily to know him."

"Then you tell me what you know," she said fiercely. "Katy, run along. I want to talk to this man alone."

Katy opened her mouth to protest, shut it again and left. When the fern doors latched, the old woman let go Dave's wrist.

"You come in here and shut that door and tell me why you think my beautiful son killed this man Oats."

"You don't want to hear it," Dave said.

"You think I'm weak," she said. "You're wrong. I'm crippled up and I'm blind. That's the Lord's will and he's blessed me a hundred other ways and I don't complain. But I'm not weak. I'm strong." Her jaw closed on the word like a trap meant to splinter bone. "If I wasn't strong, Wade would never be where he is today. Now you tell me what you know and you tell it to me straight. Who was this John Oats?"

Dave shut the door. "I'd like a drink," he said.

"If you mean whiskey, we don't keep it. Wheel me over by a chair so's you can sit."

He did. Her lined face turned toward him stoic. He told her who John Oats was, about the burns, about the morphine, about Dwight Ingalls and Sam Wald. "The day he died, he phoned them first. They both told him they weren't coming. Later they lost their nerve and did go. But he couldn't know that would happen. And he needed money. So he phoned your son. He'd held off on that a long time, probably out of love for his own son. Everyone says they were very close. But in the end, drugs don't permit you any decency."

"But—" She was very white. "He was blackmailing those other men. How could he blackmail Wade? Why would he think Wade would give him money?"

Dave took a grim breath and let it out. "Mrs. Cochran— Peter Oats is a homosexual. Do you know what that means?"

She sniffed, her mouth twitched. "I've lived a long time, mister. I've seen and heard just about everything a woman of seventy-five could be expected to, and a mite more than most. I know what you're talking about." She turned her face away. "What's it got to do with my son?"

"Maybe nothing," Dave said. "I could be wrong. But I don't think I am. He's in his thirties. He's never married. There's a lot of publicity about him in the magazines. None of it ever mentions a woman. No woman except you."

"He's attached to me," she flared. "He wouldn't hurt me by trifling with women. What other woman could have made him what I did? He's got everything a man could ask for in this world. And he's doing good with it. He's serving Jesus Christ with it. Not like the rest of them, with their drink and their night clubs and their divorces."

"Right," Dave said. "But when John Oats called, he went. Arena Blanca's fifty miles from here and it was a rainy night. But he got in that yellow Lotus of his and he went there. There's got to be a reason."

"He wasn't afraid. He's afraid of no man. He's got no cause to be afraid." Her warped fingers gripped hard on the book in her lap. "He'd seen this boy Peter in this play, you say. They'd taken supper together. It must have been to talk business. The boy's an actor."

"It wasn't the boy who called. Anyway, your son told me he wasn't interested in Peter as an actor. He pretended he hardly remembered him. He said they'd had a meal together—once. That wasn't true. Shall I tell you what I think was true?"

She didn't say yes, but she waited.

"I think your son fell in love with Peter Oats. He's beautiful and gentle. I think Peter fell in love with him. I think they slept together at that motel. And I think they wanted to go on sleeping together. It couldn't be here. But it could be up at that lodge of his, where no one goes but himself."

Her dry lips moved, but no speech came.

"The boy went home and packed his belongings. That much is fact. He talked to his father. On that I haven't the facts. His father refused to discuss it with the girl whose house he and Peter were sharing. But it upset him badly. And I think I know what it was. Peter had a weakness for honesty. He and his father had been good friends. I think he told him he was homosexual, that he'd found a man to love and was going to live with him. He gave his father the phone number here. Obviously he also gave him the name of the man—your son's name."

"Did he know his father was a dope fiend?" She was trembling. Her voice scratched like an old phonograph record. "If he did, it was a wicked thing to do. A terrible thing. He's destroyed my son."

"I think he was like you," Dave said. "If he'd paid attention, he would have noticed changes in his father, something wrong. But he loved the man and it blinded him—I'm sorry. He didn't see because he didn't want to see. No, I don't think he knew his father was an addict."

But she wasn't listening. She was grinding the words out under her breath. "Destroyed my son. My wonderful son. Destroyed him." She jerked her head up and was fierce again. "That boy can't be handsome, he can't be gentle. You're lying. He'd plotted with his father to get money out of Wade." Her jaw thrust forward, the pinched nostrils flared. "And if Wade did kill the man—"

"If he did, he didn't tell the boy. He didn't suspect any plot. He wanted to keep him. There wasn't much chance

Peter would hear of his father's death. Not shut away up there at the lodge. And when he did hear, he'd hear of an accident, a drowning. That was how Wade had arranged the murder to look. Only I didn't believe it. And I turned up here, saying I thought Peter had killed his father for his insurance. That my company wasn't accepting the verdict of death by misadventure. Wade couldn't go to the lodge right then because you had plans for him and that evangelist. And your plans for him come first. But next morning he went. What happened up there I don't know. What I do know is that in a few hours Peter walked into police headquarters in El Molino and turned himself in for the murder of his father."

He stood up and looked down on the beautiful white hair. "There's a Bible verse, Mrs. Cochran. I'm sure you know it better than I do. 'Greater love hath no man than this—'"

She didn't lift her head. She finished it tonelessly. "'That he lay down his life for his friend.'"

"Do you want me to get Katy for you?"

She shook her head. "I want to pray."

He left her like that, alone, in the middle of the handsome make-believe room, at the end of her make-believe world.

21

"It don't amount to a damn." For a tenth time Sheriff C. Clinton Hackett of Maricopa County fingered back his shirt cuff and squinted at his watch, thick steel on a thick strap on a thick wrist. He rocked in a creaky yellow swivel chair back of a yellow desk and chewed a wooden match, working it from one side of his slack mouth to the other. His eyes were little and pale and restless. He wanted to be someplace else. "A telephone call from a man who happened to drown that night, some white sand under the fenders of his car. Not a damn."

"He was a drug addict," Dave said, "and he was using blackmail. I have witnesses to that."

"No witnesses to what was said in that phone call." The Sheriff swiveled his chair half around, faced a barred window where brown tin Venetian blinds hung crooked at half-mast. Outside, birds squabbled, noisy, shrill, over sleeping rights in the dark old acacia trees that framed the parking lot of the Maricopa County Offices building. The lot was empty except for a fat five-year-old Cadillac and three brown patrol cars. "No witnesses the Oats boy was ever at Cochran's ranch."

"Check out that private lodge of his. You'll find the boy's clothes."

The Sheriff sighed and turned back. "I used to ride pretty good. Had a big bay gelding to carry me. Lot of Mexican silver mounting on the saddle. Used to go on that long ride out of Santa Barbara every year at fiesta time. Always got down to Pasadena for the Rose Parade. Then I hurt my back. Spine like a stack of broken crockery now. Be worth three months in the hospital was I to get aboard a horse today."

"Send somebody," Dave said.

Hackett wagged loose jowls. "Couldn't get no warrant. You think any judge around here would sign a warrant against Wade Cochran? Oh, they might"—something sly, meant for a smile, twitched his mouth, showing big rabbity teeth—"supposing we'd caught him up to his ass in the water, chucking Oats under and holding him there till the bubbles stopped. But nobody in this neck of the woods is going to brace a big, famous man like that on a mixed-up story like yours. About a murder somebody else already took the blame for." A snort. "They sure as hell aren't going to amble up to him and call him a pansy."

Hackett rose, all six feet seven of him. "I got to go. Get supper. Get a bath." A lower button of his starchy uniform shirt was open. It showed a parenthesis of white cotton-knit undershirt stretched taut over a massive beer belly. "Wreck-O-Rama out at the fairgrounds tonight. Drivers going to smash up a quarter-million dollars' worth of Detroit's finest. Slam 'em together, roll 'em over, bust 'em into flames." He lifted a jacket off the back of the swivel chair and hunched into it, a short jacket that might have fitted him once but was tight under the arms now and lacked the yardage to let him fasten it and zip it up. A six-pointed silver star was pinned to the breast pocket. He chuckled, pleased. "Wall-to-wall mayhem. I'm going to be master of ceremonies."

Dave stood. "Where's the County Attorney's office?"

"Up the hall." Hackett grunted, bending for a brown Stetson on a yellow chair stacked with dusty manila folders that leaked papers. "But he won't be there. It's past five."

He settled the hat on his narrow skull, tugged the brim, pulled open a door that had his name on its frosted-glass panel. "Don't nobody but prisoners and guards hang around here after five. Would you?" He wrinkled a red-veined nose. "You like the smell of this place?"

"Now that you mention it," Dave said, "no."

In the center of the night courtyard, light came up watery out of the dripping fountain. It made tremulous green ghosts of the cement Saint Francis and his doves. Around him the windows of the closed shops glowed mildly through the olive trees. Dave crossed the red tiled pavement to Oats and Norwood, thumbed the brass door latch, pushed inside, where the big globe of the world hadn't turned. Lamplight glanced off it dully, as if from a dying sun. And he saw the marks of his own fingers in the dust.

But there were customers tonight. College youngsters. A boy and girl together, he in Levi's, she in floor-length paisley. A lone boy in what looked like an old theater doorman's coat, scarlet, with gold epaulets and frogs, much too big for him. His hair was very long and he kept pushing it away from his face while he read. Charles Norwood, in his jacket with the leather patch elbows, stood by him, frowning as if trying to remember something. Eve Oats climbed down a set of movable steps with three titles for the boy and girl. When she turned from them and saw Dave, her practiced smile went away. She came to him.

"Surely you've closed this case to your satisfaction?" Her tone was arctic.

"Wrong," he said. "Peter didn't kill his father. He's covering up for the man who did." Norwood turned sharply. "What's that?"

"Please, Charles." She said it without looking at him and without inflection. She eyed Dave thoughtfully. "You're an extraordinary man. What are you talking about. Have you proof?"

"Proof is a simple word for what I've got," Dave told her. "I'd like the name of that lawyer you hired. He can make use of it. I phoned Captain Campos for the information, but he's not in. Neither is the District Attorney. I tried phoning you, but the line's been busy."

"I'm sorry. I keep thinking of things to tell the lawyer. God knows, Peter's not telling him anything."

"What's his name?" Dave said.

She shook her head. "I'm paying him. I want to hear it first. I need to hear it." Emotion shook her voice. She didn't like that. She switched to sarcasm. "It may be difficult for you to understand, but I'm just a shade concerned." The young couple went to the wrapping counter and laid down their books by the old pierced-iron cash register. She flicked them a smile. She said to Dave, "You can be comfortable in the back room. I'll try not to keep you waiting."

The room was dark. He bent and pulled the switch chain on the Tiffany lamp. It threw a shattered harlequin circle on the high ceiling, but left the corners dark. On the low, round table the light glinted off martini glasses where melt from ice cubes was drowning the olives. The books and papers hadn't been disturbed since last time. He dropped into one of the red leather chairs, lit a cigarette, then noticed the letter that had bothered him before. He reached out and picked it up.

Still baffled, he frowned through the reading glasses at the fancy London letterhead. GAYLORD AND STEEN. He ran his eye down the typing. A list of Sinclair Lewis first editions, signed, in mint condition with dust wrappers. *From Our Mr. Wrenn* to *World So Wide*. The senders were sure Mr. Oats would be interested in this superb collection of the work of a foremost twentieth-century American novelist and Nobel Prize winner. They were giving Oats and Norwood first crack at it. The books would be held for them thirty days. The price was steep.

Out in the shop the cash register jingled and clunked. Voices crossed each other with thanks and goodnights. Footsteps scuffled. The door opened and closed. Norwood's ladylike baritone said something about being sorry. The door opened and closed again. And this time Dave heard the snap of a spring lock. He glanced at his watch. Not seven yet and the lettering on the shop door said it was open till nine. He laid the booklist down, folded away his horn rims, and both of them came in.

Eve picked up the glasses and handed them to Norwood, who took them to the shadowy desk and rattled bottles there. She sat on the edge of the chair opposite Dave and held tight to the arms. She held tight to her voice too. "Now, what's this about Peter"—his wording escaped her—"sacrificing himself for someone? Who? Why? Why in the world? Oh, I don't mean it's not like him. He'd have done it for his father. But their love—"

"You told me," Dave said. "Now let me tell you." He was tired of going over it. But he went over it. He didn't skip details. Some of them made her flinch. When Norwood set a new martini in front of her she grabbed for it. The glass was stocky and tough. It needed to be. She clutched it so hard her knuckles showed white. She was white around the mouth. Dave told her about the phone call and came to the end.

"It's a nice place, five miles back through the mountains off the coast road. Just north of Las Cruces. A little valley all to itself. His car was in the yard. No mistaking that car. A Lotus. Bright yellow." Norwood got up and moved into the dark. Dave said, "It gets washed, but only by hand and not under the fenders." A desk drawer opened and shut with a loose rattle. "I checked under the fenders. Caked with white sand." Norwood walked out into the shop. Dave said, "That car was in Arena Blanca the night John Oats was drowned." The shop door opened and closed. "A rainy night. The only rainy night we've had. And Wade Cochran is a big man and a strong swimmer."

In the alley under the window a car door slammed, an engine thrashed into life. Dave stubbed out his cigarette, stood. "Now—how do I reach that lawyer?"

He was a soft, silver-haired man of seventy in an expensive shantung suit and a hand-stitched Irish linen shirt with a roll collar and deep cuffs linked by silver gavels. The carefully tended hands that came out of the cuffs were folded in front of him on the long tan steel table in the tan-walled interrogation room of the El Molino Police Department. Beside the hands a soft black hat and light black topcoat lay over a black cowhide attaché case. The man's name was Irving Blau. His voice rustled like dry leaves. "You weren't there?"

Peter Oats said, "No. He's got nothing to do with this. Yes, he came to *Lorenzaccio*. Yes, we went to dinner. Yes, we went to that motel." The brown eyes pleaded. "To talk. Only to talk. He's making a picture. It's kind of a secret project. Not like what he usually does. Not a Western. Religious. About the life of Saint Paul. He thought I could do the part. But that's nothing personal. That's business. He's got nothing to do with this."

"This is your father's writing, isn't it?" Dave pushed the yellow card across the table. "Why did he write your name down with Wade Cochran's phone number?"

"Because—because—I thought I was going there. I mean, Wade, Mr. Cochran, talked about having me up there. But he changed his plans. I never went."

"Where did you go?" Blau asked. "That can't be an important secret now, can it?"

"I don't want to get anyone in trouble."

"You've already done that," Dave said.

"I don't want to talk about it. Only just leave Wade alone. Leave him alone. He didn't do anything. I did it." The boy's fists clenched on his knees. "How many times do I have to tell you? I did it. Leave him out of it."

"He took a call from your father when your father was desperate for money to buy illegal morphine. He left the ranch right after that call. The sand under the fenders proves he drove to Arena Blanca. He'd only have done that if your father was able to threaten him with something. I've already said what I think that something was. A charge of homosexuality wouldn't harm a lot of actors. Not these days. But it would sure as hell harm Wade Cochran—to understate the case."

"You've got a rotten mind!" the boy shouted.

The door opened. Johnson, the bulky young officer with the close crew cut, looked in, scowling. "Everything all right in here?"

"Excuse us," Blau said.

Johnson glared at the boy. "Keep it down, Oats." He pulled his head out and shut the door again.

Dave said, "Bob Whittington made a pass at you. You turned him down. But for other reasons. Not because you were straight. He asked you and you told him—you weren't straight. I imagine if I asked around among the boys at that theater I could get confirmation. Couldn't I get confirmation?"

Peter swung out of the chair and stood with his back to them, hands on the sill of the dark window. "It doesn't mean anything about Wade."

"He thought it meant something," Blau said in his gentle old man's voice. "He didn't go to Arena Blanca and kill a man because it didn't mean anything."

"You'd told your father you were a homosexual," Dave said. "Isn't that right? That was why you parted on bad terms, why he drank that night, why he refused to tell April the reason you'd left."

"He hated what he called fags," Peter said in a dead voice. "He was always joking about them. Bad jokes. For a long time I didn't know why. Then, when I got older, I saw it was to get at Charles. It always made Charles uncomfortable. I think Charles was in love with my father. Much good it ever did him."

"Norwood," Dave told Blau. "The partner."

Peter's voice came bleak off the window glass. "I was slow finding out about myself. It didn't happen till—what?—a year, fourteen months ago. I was trying to work out a way to tell him when he had the accident and everything fell apart for him. I couldn't add that, knowing how he felt about it. But then there was April, somebody who loved him, somebody he could love."

"Which let you off the hook when Cochran came along and you wanted to go live with him."

"No!" The boy whirled, bent forward, fingers digging into his thighs, mouth twisting. "No. Wade isn't that way. You've got to believe me. Don't do anything to him. Oh, God, can't you see? If he did go to Arena Blanca, he didn't kill him. I killed him. For just what you said. I went to see him and he told me he was going to change his life insurance."

Dave shook his head. "The first you heard about that was after I'd been to see Cochran. He gave you the story just the way I'd given it to him."

"No. I wasn't there." Peter came to the table, leaned on it, leaned at them, veins standing out in his temples, his smooth brown throat. "Please. Promise me you'll leave Wade out of this. Forget him. Please. Why should he be hurt for nothing?" He looked at Dave. "You said it. He could be wrecked, he could lose everything. Why should he? He didn't do anything wrong. He couldn't do anything wrong. You don't know him."

"You talk like his mother," Dave said. "Peter—he had a very powerful motive. He killed your father. It took him forty-five, fifty minutes to reach Arena Blanca from the ranch. That put him there no earlier than six. It had been dark a half-hour by then. Longer because it was raining. Why he'd do it I don't know, but he had supper with your father. Two men—one highball. He doesn't drink. He keeps a clear head. It was thoughtful of him to pick up your guitar for you while he was there. A true friend."

"He didn't." Peter's fist came down on the table. "I never—" He bit his lip.

"Never what?" Blau wondered tenderly. "Never got the guitar? Well"—he pushed back his chair and stood—"it will turn up. Someplace at that ranch. The Sheriff's men will find it."

"No," the boy begged. "Don't send them there. Don't mess him up. I did it." Tears ran down his face. He stretched out trembling hands. His voice cracked. "Please! I did it."

"Then you know where the guitar is," Blau said with a quiet smile. "Where is it, Peter?" The boy only stared.

22

HE SWUNG OFF Western on to Yucca. Tree-shadowy. Cars darkly asleep at curbs and in the driveways of old frame houses where the lights were dimmed for television watching. A cat scuttled across the street on white paws and disappeared through a hedge. A lame old woman with a scarf tied over her hair dragged a wooden shopping cart on squeaky wheels along the cracked sidewalk, coming from a nearby all-night market. In the next block a thin man with a jacket hung over his shoulders held a leash while a dachshund sniffed the tarred base of a telephone pole.

Dave halted for the red tin sign at Harvard and smiled. Not much of a smile, but heartfelt. Home. Blau could handle the rest and handle it right. He could forget it. And sleep. Last night, in that white room at Madge's with the slow surf sighing under the windows, he'd got less sleep than sex. It had been good again, loving and easy, after weeks of not being good. But it had left him tired. Doug was still at Madge's, but she had a houseful of people coming tonight and Dave didn't want to cope. He touched the throttle, pulled the wheel left. He'd phone Doug as soon as he got in the back door. Then he'd hit that doomed bed and—

He tramped the brake, killed the motor, stared. Up the street, black-and-white cars stood at angles. On their tops, red lights flared, faded, flared. In the bloody pulsing of the lights, dark uniforms moved. Across the street, kids, shirt-sleeved men, women in curlers gaped. Dave woke the engine, jerked the car to a curb where mustard spread tall in a vacant lot. He got out of the car while it still rocked. The nearest officer looked about sixteen, very blond. He leaned into a patrol car whose radio droned loud in a flat female voice. He hung a dashboard microphone back on its hook.

Dave asked him, "What's going on?"

The boy didn't look at him. He waved a hand. "Stand over there, please." He started to walk off.

"That's my house," Dave said.

The boy turned back, frowning. "Let me see your identification." Dave found his wallet, slipped out of its plastic folder his driver's license, handed it to the boy. The boy tipped it to catch the greenish glare from the streetlight at the corner. He read it attentively, handed it back. His look was grim. "Where have you been?"

"Out of town. Now, will you tell me—"

One of the cars shifted position and the boy tugged Dave's sleeve to draw him out of the way. Two black officers were in the car. The one at the wheel backed it fast with a ripping sound from the transmission. When it was out of the way Dave saw the yellow Lotus. Parked directly in front of the house. Its curbside door hung open and by it squatted a muscular gray-haired man with a broken nose. He was talking to someone in the car. Dave couldn't see who it was. The headrest on the bucket seat was too high. But he knew the man.

"Ken Barker," he said. "Is he in charge?"

"He'll want to talk to you. Lieutenant?"

Barker squinted into the beating red lights. He stood, spoke again to the one in the car, stepped into the street. "Dave." He shook hands, but he didn't smile. "What did Wade Cochran want with you?"

"I'd only be guessing. That's his car. Isn't he in it? Ask him."

"He isn't in it. He's on your doorstep. Dead."

Dave felt punched in the stomach. He swung to stare at the house. Headlights glared across the ground cedar, dyeing it too green, lit up the new FOR SALE sign on its iron stem and threw hard against the front door the shadow of a uniformed officer with his head bowed. The thing at his feet wore a fringed buckskin jacket and its face was a wet glister of crimson.

"Shot three times," Barker said. "The weapon was small-caliber, but the range was close. Why, Dave?"

Dave gave him a frail smile. "For our sins, Ken." He looked at the Lotus. "He brought his mother, right?"

Barker nodded. "But she can't tell us anything. She's blind. Cochran got out of the car. She heard him go up the walk. He's wearing cowboy boots. This is a quiet street. She heard your door buzzer. Then another car pulled up, the door slammed, feet ran up the walk. Cochran said, "No," just once. The gun went off three times. The killer ran back to his car and drove away. The old lady leaned on the horn. Couple of neighbors came. They phoned us." Barker checked his watch. "Twenty minutes ago. She could be away from here by now. She won't budge. She wants to talk to you. Said she'd wait all night if necessary."

She sat stiff-backed, stoic, used to pain, stronger than pain. What ought to have been under her was a buckboard seat. Her raw dignity made the car's padded leather, glittering dials and gauges, sleek curve of windshield look ridiculous. Dave crouched in the ground cedar, touched her, told her who he was.

She turned. "You got here."

"Too late," he said. "I'm sorry."

"Not your fault. He wanted to phone ahead. I said no phoning. We'll go. They listen in on phones all the time these days. We'll talk to him face to face." She lifted her head. "Barker, you still there?"

"Yes, ma'am." He stood behind Dave. "Well, go away. Find my son's killer."

"Everyone's looking for him," Barker said. "I have to hear what you're going to say."

"All you have to hear is that killer's name and I don't know it." Her gnarled hand caught Dave's. "You get into this car."

Dave stood and looked at Barker. A nerve twitched in Barker's face, but he didn't speak. He looked stonily at Dave. His gunmetal eyes said, *You'll tell me later.* Dave didn't nod. He held Barker's look for a slow count of three. Barker could make whatever he wanted out of that. Dave went around and got behind the wheel of the Lotus. His door fell shut. He reached across and shut her door.

"This can't be kept quiet," he said. "There'll be newsmen here in five minutes."

"What I've got to say can be kept quiet," she said.

"Maybe. I don't need to ask why he came here. He came because you made him come. What was he going to tell me?"

"That the boy didn't kill his father." She stared straight ahead at nothing. The red lights winked off the flat back of the glasses. "He was up at the lodge."

"But Wade wasn't. He went to Arena Blanca."

"Prepared to pay," she said. "There's stairs. He climbed them. It was cold and raining, but the door was open. He looked inside. The lights was on. Plates on the table, meal just et. Coffee still steaming in the cups. Cigarette smoking in the ashtray. But nobody there. He called out, but nobody come. Well, I trained him better than to go into somebody's place when they're not home. He went down and waited in the car. But not for long. Afraid he'd be seen. He come back to the ranch.

"And rode up to the lodge. The boy was there, but Wade didn't tell him where he'd been and why. It was like you claimed it was between them. Love, you called it. I can't accept that. Bible doesn't and I can't. Lived my whole life by the Word of God. Raised him by it. He knew better, knew he was in the wrong—otherwise he'd have spoken to me about it. But that's not here nor there now.

"What is, is that this man John Oats says his son told him he was going to live with Wade and why—just like you guessed. Threatened to tell. Unless Wade brought him money. Wade was sure the boy never knew his father was a dope fiend." She gave a little dry laugh that had only despair in it. "Like you said about me. Love don't let you doubt. *Believeth all things.* First Corinthians, thirteen, seven."

"I think he was right. The boy didn't know."

"Mebbe." She clipped the word short. "I can't like him. You can't ask me to like him. My son was all right till he come along. He was fine. Just fine. The whole world thought so." Her voice trembled and went old-woman thin. "And now look what's happened. Look how it's ended."

"The boy tried to save him," Dave said.

"Because it was his fault and he knew it. He thought Wade had killed his father. Oh, yes." Her smile was crooked, triumphant. "If it was love, it ended right then and there. The day you first come to the ranch. Wade sized you up. You wouldn't stop till you found that boy. And tracking him, you'd find where they ate, that motel where they lay together in abomination. You didn't say anything about the dope, the blackmail, but you'd find out about them too. And come back."

"He could have washed under those fenders."

Curt headshake. "That wouldn't have stopped you. Not once you learned about the phone call from John Oats. He didn't know where to turn. Every time he'd had trouble in his life before, there'd been his mother to talk to. He couldn't talk to me about this. The boy was all he had. And the boy thought he did it. But"—the twist of her smile was bitter— "he couldn't let Wade take the blame. Not seeing he'd brought the trouble. *He'd* take the blame. There was no point in living now, anyways."

"And Wade would have let him," Dave said. "If it hadn't been for you, Wade would have let him go straight to the gas chamber."

"But the boy was wrong!" Her cry had a crow's harshness. "Wade didn't do it. You know that now. Somebody else did it. The same one that shot Wade."

"Right." Dave found the door handle, lifted it, pushed the door open. "The same one." With a low siren moan, an ambulance edged its way around the cluster of black-and-white cars. It was a tall brown carryall. On its roof a wan orange light revolved under a plastic blister. The machine tilted clumsily into the driveway, followed by an unmarked car with a whip antenna. Men in white jumped down from the ambulance cab and in the headlight beams of the second car opened the rear doors to slide out an aluminum-tubing stretcher and a bulky fold of gray plastic, a sack for the dead. They headed for the front door. From the unmarked car a round-shouldered man with a small black grip trudged after them—Grace of the coroner's office. From the same car two men followed, trampling the ground cedar, carrying camera, lights and glittering, spidery tripods.

Dave got out of the Lotus, then turned back, bent, poked his head inside. "You said he was afraid he'd been seen. That night in the rain at Arena Blanca."

"He wasn't," she said. "He told me he wasn't."

"He was," Dave said. "Shall I phone Katy for you?"

She set her jaw. "I'll stay here with my son."

But she wouldn't. As he straightened, Dave saw a mannish young woman in trim uniform get out of a newly arrived patrol car. She came toward the Lotus with a look of gentle firmness. Dave shut the door and glanced around for Barker. The white flashes of the cameraman's strobes outlined him, near the body, watching the crouched doctor. Dave started toward him, then halted. To hell with him. He didn't have jurisdiction in El Molino. He could wait. Dave made for his car.

A stocky man who looked anxious came fast along the sidewalk. A milkweed stalk clung to the cuff of his pants. He'd picked it up crossing the vacant lot. Dave saw his car around the corner, white, marked with radio-station call letters. ALL THE NEWS ALL THE TIME. A tape recorder in a scuffed leather case bounced at the man's hip. He waved a shiny microphone.

"Excuse me. Our man at the Glass House got the flash Wade Cochran's been shot to death. The TV star. Do you know anything about it? Whose house is that?"

"Grandmother's." Dave kept walking. "Only there was a wolf in the bed."

He slammed inside his car, started it, yanked the lever to reverse. He floored the gas pedal and the tires screamed, caught, jerked the car backward along the curb to the empty cross street, where he cramped the wheel, cornered, braked so the tires shouted again. And a third time when he set the lever to drive and took off along Yucca. A glance over his shoulder told him no one in the red-light nightmare had noticed. Not even the reporter. He was arguing with the towheaded kid in uniform.

23

IT WAS BACK in the dark, fourth on the left in a jogged row of one-story apartments. Sharp-edged pale stucco, neat and ungenerous. Clean, short cement steps up to aluminum screen doors. White-painted wood doors with beveled panels. White Venetian blinds at the windows. But no light inside. Not at number four. Only the imbecile insistence of a telephone, ringing, ringing.

Dave walked out to the street again. A narrow cement strip led back of the apartments. He used it. The shiny screen on the back door of number four was unlatched, but the half-glass door inside it was locked. While his hand was on the knob the telephone stopped. He went on out to an alley. The only light was the pale reflection in the sky of lights from a business street two blocks away, but it let him see to his right a row of car stalls, open crates of blackness.

He laid a hand on the hood of a Galaxy, of a Chevelle, on the rear slope of a Volkswagen. Cold. Then he heard small sounds. Two cars farther on. A little old Sunbeam with a worn fold-down roof. *Tick. Ping.* The engine bonnet was warm. He pulled open the rusty little door, lit a match, leaned inside to check the registration slip in its yellowed celluloid folder on the steering post. Yes. He blew out the match.

He shut the door, took a step, crouched, reached up under a fender, scraped with his nail, stood and moved out into the alley. He held his open hand close to his eyes. The white sand grains glittered. He brushed them away, bent and tried the corrosion-rough handle of the Sunbeam's luggage compartment. It didn't turn easy, it turned with a squeak, but it turned. He lifted the lid. Nothing inside but a spare tire and tools.

At the back of the car stalls, built high so that the grilles of the cars could nose under, was a row of storage lockers, unpainted tongue-and-groove boards. Padlocked. He picked up the Sunbeam's tire iron, edged between the little car and the Mustang next to it, raised the jimmy and pried at the cheap hasp. The pine was soft. The hasp gave, the padlock rattled, the screws pattered on the cement at his feet. He opened the door.

Matchlight flickered yellow on old books bundled with twine. Cardboard cartons jaundiced with age and damp. A dusty Tyrolean hat of checkered green, in its band a clip of red feather that had once been jaunty. A dry pair of leather motoring gloves with holes at the fingertips, bent to a grasp, as if there were hands still in them. Dribbled cans of enamel, varnish, thinner. A clutch of used paintbrushes. A dented red ten-gallon gasoline tin.

And a guitar.

The telephone was ringing when he reached the back door again. The lock was the kind that twists inside a brass knob. He used the jimmy gently to pry loose the flat wood strip on the right side of the doorframe. Just a crack. The telephone stopped. From his wallet he took a plastic-coated card, calendar on one side, ad for whiskey on the other. He slid this in where he'd loosened the strip, eased it between the catch and the tongue of the lock, nudged the door open. A loose metal weather strip along its bottom ticked like a dollar alarm clock.

"Who's there?" Dim to his right, light came on.

He went toward it fast between the shadowy outlines of stove, refrigerator, counters. A room divider, wood veneer cut with fleur-de-lis and sprayed gold, separated a dining space with ferns and twinkling cut glass from a living room upholstered in yellow plush. Next to the divider was width for passage. Charles Norwood stood there. Coatless, no shoes, no glasses, hair a fuzzy nimbus around his head. And in his hand a snipe-nosed .22 target pistol. His voice sounded choked.

"What the hell does this mean?"

"It means you thought Wade Cochran saw you the night you drowned John Oats. He didn't. He didn't see anyone. You killed him for nothing."

"But he turned on his headlights just as I came around the corner of the house. Naked. Dripping wet. I walked right into them. And he drove away before I—"

"Could see who he was, right? And you've been wondering ever since who owned that yellow Lotus. Sick with worry that he'd hear what happened down there that night and come forward and say he'd seen you. But there was nothing ·you could do about it. Till I walked in the bookstore tonight and told you the man's name and where to find him and that he knew about John Oats's murder.

"Then you didn't waste any time. You got that gun out of the desk. Within four feet of me and I didn't understand. As fast as you could move and not attract notice, you were out of that shop, into your car and on your way to Wade Cochran's ranch. Scared to death that once the police began trying to pin the murder on him, he'd tell about seeing you there, fresh out of the surf, right at the time it happened. Why didn't you kill him at the ranch?"

"How do you know where I killed him?"

"Oh, it's on the news," Dave said. "But I didn't need the news. It happened at my house. He wanted to see me. But not to tell me about you. Just to tell me Peter didn't do it, that Peter was at his place when it happened. I arrived home twenty minutes too late. Twenty minutes after you and your little gun departed."

"It's big enough," Norwood said. "As you're going to see. But not till we've talked. You've been so stupid about this whole thing. I want you to know just how stupid you have been. Before I shoot you for breaking and entering."

"Not with that gun," Dave said. "You want to throw that gun away. You don't want the police comparing the slugs in me with the slugs in Wade Cochran and tying them all to your toy there. And they would. The El Molino police and the Los Angeles police both know I'm in the middle of this case. You ought to have tossed that gun off the freeway coming back here. Just as you ought to have got rid of that guitar of Peter's."

"Yes. Yes, you're right." The light was back of him. His face was shadowed. But Dave saw a tight glint of teeth. The voice went oily. "Thank you. That's excellent advice. You're thoughtful. No"—sharply—"don't move. Just stand the way you are."

"I'd like a cigarette," Dave said.

"Perhaps later," Norwood said. "At the beach, before you take your swim. Like John Oats. But with guitar accompaniment."

"Very funny," Dave said. "How are we going to get to the beach?"

"You're going to drive me. I'll be in the back. Of your car, of course. With this"—light slid orange along the black gun barrel as he jerked it—"close to your ear. And while, as you suggest, it might be unwise of me to shoot you, the outcome for me can't be your primary concern. Your primary concern, being human, will be to go on breathing as long as possible. Am I right?"

"You didn't get to the ranch," Dave said.

"No. I saw that car on the freeway, ten, fifteen miles this side of Las Cruces. Heading south. I found an off ramp and an on ramp. I broke all kinds of speed limits to catch him, but after that it wasn't any strain to keep him in sight, even though my car is old and asthmatic and his could go a hundred-twenty. He was obeying the laws. I don't watch television. I prefer fine music. Perhaps that's why I didn't destroy the guitar—I couldn't bear to think of silencing anything capable of beauty. In any case, he plays a character without blemish, as I understand it. And he tries to live up to it. Tried."

"He wouldn't have wanted a ticket. Not this trip."

"It was a long, long way," Norwood complained. "Clear to the middle of Los Angeles. Over a hundred miles, did you know that? I thought he never would stop. But he did. At last he did."

"Completely," Dave said. "Like John Oats. Let's see if I'm as stupid as you think. You killed him for the insurance. In order to buy a collection of Sinclair Lewis first editions for a new Oats and Norwood catalog. The shop was going broke. You needed a good item to get back your former customers, the ones who lost interest when John Oats left.

"The letter from London quoting those books lay on the table in the back room of the shop. It took me time to remember where I'd seen the logo before. On an envelope lying with the plates from John Oats's last supper on the coffee table at April Stannard's. I saw it the first time I went there. And this afternoon in John Oats's desk I ran across a list of prices in British money. He'd added up the cost of those books while you sat there eating his food, getting ready to kill him. You thought Eve would collect his life-insurance money. And you knew she'd invest it in the shop."

"Eve told you that," Norwood said. "But she was wrong." He sounded smug. "I'd known since the morning of the day I—of the day he died that he'd made Peter his beneficiary when Eve started divorce proceedings. He told me himself. I'd telephoned him about that letter from Gaylord and Steen. It was a big investment. I'd have to borrow from the bank. I wanted his advice as to whether it was worthwhile. He asked for the prices, totaled them while we were on the phone. That's the memo you found. He advised me to go ahead.

"He was pleased to hear from me. We hadn't spoken for nearly a year. He needed to talk and he talked. It was about Peter. He was depressed and angry and hurt. Peter had left him. That was surprising in itself. I'd have bet he never would. They'd always adored each other. Then he told me why. That Peter was homosexual—that wasn't John's word, I won't repeat his word—and had gone to live with some man. Of course, it had to be something like that. Otherwise he'd have unburdened his heart to darling April. But a man like John doesn't discuss such matters with his woman. Still, he was going to leave her his money. Rub Peter's name out. He'd already phoned your company for the necessary forms. He wasn't thinking of dying, but when he did, April was going to get all he had left in the world to give. She was the only one who deserved it now."

"But you didn't agree. You don't like April."

"Who told you that? Why wouldn't I like her?"

"She told me. She said you were jealous of her. I wasn't quite sure what she meant. Till Peter made it clear. You're homosexual yourself and you've always been in love with John Oats. You'd hoped that when Eve left him it would be your turn. Oh, you knew his bias, but you couldn't let yourself believe there was no chance for you. Even if he did tell limp-wristed jokes to upset you."

"He only did that in front of others," Norwood said angrily. "He was my friend, my dear friend. When Peter was born he gave him my name. He'd never have done anything deliberately to hurt me. I understood. Telling those jokes was a way of asserting his masculinity, that's all. Trying to show anyone who might suspect me that there was nothing between us."

"And there wasn't, was there?" Dave said. "He was straight as a desert highway. You never stood a chance. It was all fantasy with you—twenty-five years of hoping against hope. Basing it mainly on the fact that Eve was a bitch and he'd get tired of her finally and turn to someone who really loved him. And you were right. Except that the someone turned out to be April, not you. And you didn't give a damn anymore what happened to him. If he'd been able to work, if he was still your partner, at least you'd have as much of him as you'd ever had. But even that was finished now. He was no use to you anymore."

"Not alive." Norwood's voice was cold. "But dead he was worth twenty thousand dollars. I thought of that when the bank turned down my application for a loan. Not that I needed that much for the Lewis books. But it was take that or nothing. And I had to take it quickly, while Peter was still the beneficiary. I sold insurance as a young man. I know what happens when a beneficiary kills to gain from a policy. The company can go to law and win sanction not to pay. On the other hand, payment has to be made to someone. The logical someone in Peter Oats's case would be his mother."

"If Peter killed his father."

"Right. And the coincidence was inviting. I didn't know you then. But I knew that if John drowned under suspicious circumstances after applying for a form to change beneficiaries, there'd be an investigator of some description on the scene. And I knew whom he'd blame for the murder. It would be so obvious. Peter—who else? Peter, in danger of losing the only inheritance his father had left to give him. And you"—Norwood's voice was heavy with contempt—"you fell for it."

"The missing guitar helped," Dave said.

"Yes, that was a nice touch—I have to admit it. But even nicer, I thought, was the single highball glass. Peter didn't drink, whereas I have never been known to turn down anything alcoholic. I simply washed my own glass and put it away where it belonged. That was very bad food, canned something or other. With ketchup, of all things. They were living on nothing. John can't have liked that. He was better off out of it. In so many—"

Keys rattled. The front door swung open. Eve Oats stepped in. "Charles, you are here. Why didn't you answer the phone? Do you know what's happened?"

Norwood had turned. Dave took a step and chopped at his wrist. The gun fell. Dave put his foot on it. Norwood swung at him with a wild backhand left. Dave tilted away from it, then drove a fist into the bookman's soft belly. He doubled over and dropped, clutching himself. Dave picked up the .22.

Eve Oats said, "What in the world?"

"Phone the police," Dave said.

*Continue reading for a preview of the next
Dave Brandstetter novel*

TROUBLEMAKER

SHE WORE JEANS, high-top work shoes, an old pullover with
a jagged reindeer pattern. Somebody's ski sweater once,
somebody even bigger than she was. Her son? She was sixty
but there was nothing frail about her. The hands gripping
the grainy rake handle were a man's hands. Her cropped
hair was white. She wore no makeup. Her skin was ruddy,
her eyes bright blue. *Hearty* might have described her. Except
for her mouth. It sulked. Something had offended her and
failed to apologize. Not lately—long ago. Life, probably. He
said, "Mrs. Wendell?" and held out a card. She took it, read
it. It named the insurance company he worked for, Medallion
Life. His own name, David Brandstetter, was in a corner,
DEATH CLAIMS DIVISION under it. He didn't try to say it.
His throat was dry. The morning was hot. It had been a hike
from Pinyon Trail up crooked steps in a steep, pine-grown
slope—rusty needles slippery underfoot—to the rambling
redwood house where no one answered the bell, then out
back here to this one-time garage.

It was a kind of stable now. Beside it, in pine-branch-
splintered sunlight, a sorrel gelding no longer young
nosed a heap of alfalfa back of an unpainted paddock
fence. A cleated board ramp fronted the garage doors,

canted to reach a wood floor laid on studs over the original cement. Inside, Heather Wendell raked manure and trampled straw out of a stall. In farther stalls, shadowy horses breathed and shifted hoofs on hollow planks. The big woman pushed the card into a pocket, turned away, went on with her work.

"Murders," she said, "inquests, grief. They don't mean anything to horses." It was a man's voice. Not pleased. "What is it you want?"

"Your son, Richard, had a policy with us."

"At my insistence." She jerked a nod, grim but self-satisfied. "He'd never have thought of it. It wasn't that he was selfish. He simply had no imagination. It never entered his head that he could die. I'd be destitute today. Well, I've had that, thank you. From my father. I wasn't going through it again. Not at my time of life." Her thick elbow nudged Dave. "Excuse me." She raked the pile past his feet, paused, blinked at him. "You've brought the check—is that it?"

"Wrong department." Dave smiled apology. "My department asks questions."

She grunted and began raking again, out into the light. She traded the rake for a stump of broom and pushed the waste off the ramp to the side. "There were a dozen police officers, in and out of uniform. That night, the next day. At least half of them asked questions. The same questions. Over and over again."

She leaned the broom beside the rake against a stud-and-board wall. Above sawhorses that held saddles, a tangle of tack trailed from rusty spikes. She took down a bridle and carried it to the stall beyond the one she'd cleaned. A bit clinked against teeth, a buckle tongue snapped. She led out a little paint mare who threw her head and blew when she saw Dave.

"Step back in there a minute, would you? Men make Buffy nervous. Thank you."

She held the sidling Buffy by a cheek strap and shouldered her out of the door. Rusty hinges creaked on the paddock gate. It closed with a wooden clatter. She came back in and took the rake to Buffy's stall.

"I assume one of those officers was bright enough to write. That Japanese one, surely. Or don't the police let insurance companies see their reports?"

"Lieutenant Yoshiba," Dave said. "I saw the report."

"Good. Then there's no need to waste your morning. Nor mine. These horses haven't been groomed or exercised in days. That's not right. And I'm pressed for time. The funeral's this afternoon."

"You'd gone to a film that night," Dave said. "In Los Santos. Left here a little after seven. The film screened at eight and ran three hours but you were back here before ten and it's a forty-minute drive. What happened?"

"I walked out. The movie was disgusting. They're all like that now—cruel, bloody, degenerate. I tried to make myself stay, it cost so much to get in. And Rick keeps telling me I'm letting myself get old, stuck away up here, that I ought to get out in civilization once in a while." The rake clunked at the back of the dark stall. She snorted. "Civilization! Do you know what they do to horses in those pictures? The SPCA here in the States won't let them use trip wires—you know, to make them stumble and fall. But they go out of the country now to film, and they don't care. They break their legs, their necks, kill them. To make a cheap, sordid movie. Don't talk to me about civilization."

"I won't," Dave said. "You got home around ten?"

"Parked the car where I always do. Down below, by the mailbox. You can see we don't use the garage for cars any more." The rake quit a moment while she jerked a thumb over her shoulder. "When we did, we drove down from the trail above—same trail but it climbs and bends back on itself. Only take horses up and down the driveway now. Hardly a patch of blacktop left on it. Anyway, the climb up the steps is good exercise. My father always said, 'Walking is for horses,' and he died at forty-nine."

"Right," Dave said. "You heard a shot?"

"When I was partway up the stairs. Didn't know what it was. Sounded like a backfire from down on the main road. These hills echo so. And my mind wasn't on it. I was furious about that movie." Now she backed past Dave again, dragging the litter from Buffy's stall with the rake. "I set some milk in a pan on the stove to heat. To calm me down, let me sleep. I thought I'd change for bed while it warmed up and I started for my room. And I saw across the way there was a light in Rick's den. That wasn't right—he was at work. Then I remembered his VW was down by the mailbox when I'd parked. Shows you how that movie upset me. Normally he doesn't get home till three." She added without pride, "It's a bar he owns, you know. With Ace Kegan."

"The Hang Ten," Dave said. "A gay bar. On Ocean Front Walk in Surf."

"Yes." She eyed him thoughtfully for a second, then went on scraping the stall muck towards the sunlit doorway. "Well, I was afraid Rick must be ill. I thought I'd better step across and check. It's a separate unit, you understand. It was a guesthouse originally—two bedrooms and bath. Rick remodeled one room so as to have a place where he could relax, listen to music, watch TV and not disturb me. Our hours are different. Were. The door was open. And there was this boy, this creature—what's his name?—Johns. Standing at the desk, stark naked, tissues in his hand, wiping off a revolver. While my son lay dead at his feet."

"Also stark naked," Dave said.

"No." She stopped in the doorway, a bulky silhouette, and raised her head. Against the light, he couldn't read her expression. But her voice changed. It belonged to an old woman now. "There was a great, gaping hole in his chest. I remember that. Was he naked? Yes." Her shoulders sagged. "I suppose he was."

"Can I see that room?" Dave asked.

"The police took photographs." The rake handle knocked the wall. She broomed the dirty straw. Angry now. Probably at herself for showing human weakness. "They left the fireplace littered with those ugly little burned-out bulbs."

"I've seen the photographs," Dave said. "Now I need to see the room. Don't stop what you're doing. Just point me the way." Wincing against the hard light, he started down the ramp.

She squared herself in front of him. "I'm not sure I have to do that. What is it you want here? No—don't bother to lie. I know insurance companies. I got acquainted with them in 1937. When all the policies my father had kept up for years were canceled. Because he'd missed some payments at the end. When he was helplessly ill. You'd like to find a way to stop my getting the money my son meant for me to have. To go on with. Lord knows, twenty-five thousand is little enough these days. Would you care to try to live the rest of your life on that amount?"

"No," Dave said. "There's going to be a delay, though, Mrs. Wendell. Till after the trial. You understand that."

She stared. "Indeed I do not. Why? The police know that boy did it. The district attorney knows."

"A jury has to know," Dave said. "Beyond a reasonable doubt. And juries aren't predictable."

"But there he stood with the gun!" she cried. "The gun that killed my son." Her lip trembled and she bit it sharply.

"Your son's own gun, wasn't it? You told the police he kept it in his desk."

"Hippies infest this canyon." She stepped past him into the stable dark. Tack jingled. She was taking another bridle off its nail. "We're isolated up here. Help's a long way off. Nowhere, if the telephone's out. And that happens, you know." Her work shoes thumped the planks. Her voice came muffled from the back of the stable. "Los Santos hasn't the most up-to-date equipment. A rainstorm, a Santana—it breaks down." A small window showed grimy light above the farthest stall. He saw her lifted hands work the bridle over a big, dark muzzle. "It would be foolish not to keep a gun up here."

"Guns are for television actors," Dave said. "Not real people. The wrong ones always get hurt. Your son could be alive this morning."

She didn't answer. She spoke to the horse, coaxing, soft. Hoofs came on, a halting stumble. Dave stepped down on to the pine-needle mat of the yard and watched her steer this one into the paddock. Ganted, knob-kneed, mane and tail stringy. The sun showed newly healed scars along sides and flanks. A rip between the eyes was still jagged and red. Heather Wendell closed the gate and over it stroked a hammer head, "Beaten with barbed wire," she said. "By a crazy man. The county would have destroyed him. Not the man—oh, never. The horse. I couldn't let them do that. He'll be all right soon." There was crooning tenderness in the words. Not for Dave. For the horse. She turned to face Dave again and he told her:

"It's not the only thing, but the gun worries me. The jury's going to snag on it too. A police lab man will tell them there were powder burns on your son's hand. And his chest. It was fired point-blank. They could come up with suicide."

"But the coroner's jury didn't say so."

"They said Johns had to stand trial. That's all. It doesn't bind the jury that will hear his case. They won't even know about it. And if they acquit Johns, it complicates things for my company. If Richard Wendell took his own life, we can't pay. It's in the policy."

"Yes." Her mouth twisted in a sour smile. "And that would suit your company, wouldn't it?" She bunched her fists. "Well, it won't happen. It's not common sense. A man doesn't commit suicide with someone else present. A stranger." She stepped towards Dave and her words came like thrown rocks. "The explanation for the powder burns is obvious. Rick was holding the gun. Probably found the boy trying to steal. They struggled. The gun went off. Right against Rick's chest."

"Maybe," Dave said. "Johns tells it a little differently." The sun beat down. Dave shed his jacket, hung it over an arm. "He claims they were in bed and Richard Wendell heard a sound in the den. He went to investigate. Johns heard voices—your son's, another man's—and a shot. He was frightened and it took him a minute to move. When he came out of the bedroom, your son lay on the floor. He bent over him, shook him. No sign of life. Blood. The gun. He picked it up because he was too dazed to be careful. Then he realized he'd made a mistake and what he had to do was wipe his prints off it, get his clothes, and run. Only the clock ran out on him. You walked in."

"And took the gun away from him." Her mouth twitched contempt. "Six feet tall, one of those long moustaches, long hair. He cried like a girl, begged, pleaded. Oh, I heard his story. Half a dozen times while he waited for the police." Her laugh was brief and scornful. "Lies. Pointless. He killed Rick."

"For money?" Dave asked. "Your son's wallet lay on the chest in his bedroom, undisturbed. Two hundred dollars in it. Ones, fives, tens, twenties."

"In case they ran short of change at The Hang Ten," she said. "He always carried it. Of course, it was there. The boy hadn't taken it because there wasn't time. I interrupted him."

"What about the open door?" Dave said. She looked blank and he told her, "You found the door open, remember? What they were doing they wouldn't leave the door open for, would they? They wouldn't only have closed it, they'd have locked it."

"There's no lock," she said. "There is—but there's no key. And the spring lock's painted shut. This is an old place. When we bought it, there wasn't any need for locks up here. Too remote. And we had Homer, our big Dane. Dead now."

"But it was standing open," Dave said. "That's going to help Johns's defense."

"He has no defense," she said flatly. "He'd opened it himself and left it open and Rick heard him out there and came out and—"

"Naked?" Dave said gently.

"I don't know what that means," she said, "but he's a hippie. They're all over up here. Why hadn't he wandered in? Who knows what goes on in their heads? It's common knowledge they've ruined their minds with drugs. He didn't come by car. At least the police haven't found a car."

"He says your son picked him up and brought him here," Dave said. "And his clothes weren't in the den, Mrs. Wendell. They were in the bedroom."

She opened her mouth and shut it hard and turned to tramp off up the board slope into the stable. "I have work to do." When she came out, her big fingers clasped a square wood-backed brush, a coarse-toothed metal comb that glinted in the sunlight. She let herself into the paddock and began working on the sorrel.

Dave walked to the fence, put a foot up on the lowest bar, crossed his arms on the top bar and rested his chin on them. "I went to the theatre last night," he said. "In Los Santos. Talked to the night crew. You're not somebody who'd go unnoticed, Mrs. Wendell. Nobody remembers seeing you."

The brush stopped its motion. She turned. "Mr. Brandstetter, my fingerprints are also the only ones on that gun. Neither circumstance means anything. Since you don't appear to have the wit to see that, I shall explain it to you. My son earned twelve to fourteen thousand dollars a year. Gave me a roof over my head, clothes for my back, food to eat. He let me indulge my hobby, which is an expensive one. Not without protest—but he never in the end denied me anything. Now . . . why would I kill him? For twenty-five thousand dollars insurance money?"

"It doesn't add up," Dave admitted. "Neither does anything else about this case. That's what bothers me." He sighed, straightened, turned from the fence. "But it will. It will." He looked down at the gray shake roofs tree-shadowed below. "Are those his rooms, in the L of the house there?"

Joseph Hansen (1923–2004) was the author of more than twenty-five novels, including the twelve groundbreaking Dave Brandstetter mystery novels. The winner of the 1992 Lifetime Achievement Award from the Private Eye Writers of America, Hansen was also the author of *A Smile in his Lifetime, Living Upstairs, Job's Year,* and *Bohannon's Country.* He was a two-time Lambda Literary Award-winner.